TABLE OF C...

Dedication

To the Memory of Lois Jean

Grateful for her support & passion for reading during my life inspiring me to a love for literature.

Acknowledgements

Don't Judge a Book... was a labor of perseverance lasting over years of revisiting and modifications. Francesca's story of her struggles to overcome numerous traumas continued to lead her to addictions and other toxic alternatives. Her journey to tranquility may never cease before she pays the ultimate price.

To Jonathan Haupt and Suzie Webster: Thank you for your professional guidance and supportive friendship.

To Dre, James, Lisa, Margaret, and my son, Alex: Thank you for inspiring the character development and unconditional presence in my life.

To Sista Cynthia and Marti: Thank you for being the best Beta Readers and being a supportive foundation of my family.

To Savannah: Thank you for your counseling expertise and friendship.

To Sharon Blake, CEO Life Chronicles Publishing: Thank you for your virtual hand holding in navigating me thru a debut novel. You and your editor's patience and talents are admirable.

To Darius Harris, Design Manager Life Chronicles Publishing: Thank you for your amazing design in portraying my vision for Francesca and Damien's story.

CHAPTER
ONE

From his wheelchair, John bellowed his response, "No!" as he lunged at her.

Francesca's cry of, "Stop!" radiated through the hallway. She jumped back and barely moved clear of hitting the wall.

Dr. Scott Barber and several male interns heard her distress call and came running to her rescue. They were able to restrain John until his medication took effect.

"Are you alright?" Dr. Barber inquired.

"I'm not hurt. I was just caught off guard," Francesca responded with embarrassment.

"Did the patient have any history of being aggressive?" Dr. Barber asked in order to be proactive and prevent any further abrupt actions.

"I was in the beginning of his evaluation. His sister stated he had a history of depression but no aggressive behavior. Last semester I had been exposed during my Research Practicum to violent patients. I'm sorry I didn't pick up on this one!" Francesca tried not to show her true emotions.

"These things happen to even the most seasoned professional. Don't beat yourself up over it. Use it as a learning experience. Finish the incident report and then take a break." Dr. Barber had always been a compassionate mentor towards her. She had felt he was a true father figure for the students.

Francesca thought she could read a patient's mood. However, this one caught her completely by surprise with his unpredictable meltdown. She was off duty, exhausted from clinicals at the Adult Behavioral Unit. Francesca had three months left and was anxious for the completion of a degree for her December 1994 graduation.

Francesca took the Doctor's Walkway exit outside. She proceeded to the garage towards the elevator and the stairwell's glass enclosure. Francesca felt she was being watched and decided to take the stairs to Level 3, where she had parked. She prayed it was paranoia. Her theory was not to be trapped in an elevator with anyone. The hospital parking garage had been quiet except for the noisy traffic on Ralph McGill Boulevard that bounced off the low ceiling and the occasional ambulance arrivals to Georgia Baptist Hospital.

In the stairwell, the sounds of heavy footsteps below her were getting faster and closer. As she approached the doorway to Level 3, she could see her car parked halfway up the uncovered ramp on the right. She had to make a split decision. Francesca wasn't an athletic person, but she was healthy. She was in her mid-thirties and had a full-figured body. She decided it would be best to go up the ramp to the left to hide. If this person caught her on the right, her fear was he might throw her off the roof. Her breathing was more rapid as her pace was increasing to a run as she exited the stairwell. She tripped; her body hit the pavement. Francesca's chest felt as though it would explode with the violent beating of her heart. She didn't comprehend the extent of her injuries. Hid towards the back bumper, she was only able to crawl a few cars up the ramp. The desperation was consuming her whole body.

As Francesca tried to catch her breath and keep her body still, numerous questions flashed through her mind. Who was this person and why were they chasing her? She wondered if the mysterious envelope that was delivered to her front door was involved. The written message was "You will pay for what has been done to me!" She wanted to remember the details for the article about the hit and run victim that was attached, this meant the same thing would happen to her. Maybe her ex, Kenny was right and a past love interest had become a stalker. She wished she had informed her lawyer brother, Brian so he could protect her.

Francesca heard the footsteps go past the car then crawled to the front end. She was brushing her hair from her face. Francesca was reaching down to touch her bloody knees through her torn pants. She immediately was feeling a painful tingling sensation. She wasn't sure if she would make it or not then decided to try to escape to the stairs. Francesca stood and began bolting towards the stairwell located behind the doorway to the elevator. Safety would be within her grasp. Just as she was about to take her first step down, she felt a sharp pain in her back and was being thrown over the left railing. Before she had a chance to react, Francesca's face hit the concrete steps with a violent force. Her eyes shut while blacking out before she tumbled down the remainder of the stairs.

She awoke to pain throughout her entire body and attempted to pull herself to the doorway of Level 2. Her face felt as if it were a shattered jigsaw puzzle as blood streamed down one cheek. The other side of her face was numb, and she could barely see out of her eye. She was gasping for air and having difficulty breathing through her broken nose. The sound of curdling blood erupted through her lungs. As the echo in the stairwell rang out she could no longer tolerate the extreme pain and lost consciousness.

CHAPTER TWO

Francesca Stefani was busy working for a public relations firm in Atlanta while on weekends finishing her clinical rotations to be a psychologist. At the age of 33, she never seemed to have much free time for herself or male companionship. She has a best friend named Angie Tyler and a cat named Dizzy Gillespie. Angie was a few months older than Francesca and they had been friends most of their lives. Angie was a full-figured blonde who was divorced with three kids and lived in a small town a couple of hours north of Atlanta.

After returning home from one of her hospital shifts, Francesca began browsing through the Atlanta Constitution Newspaper when she came across the personals section. She chuckled as she read some of the ads which she knew had to be a part of the writer's imagination. Since her friends had been concerned about the lack of love life, she submitted an ad to the Personals. Francesca called Angie since she knew she would jump at

7

the chance to give input on this mission to find the right mate. She never thought in 1994 the dating craze would be the newspaper personals. After several revisions, the ad was ready.

Looking for Mr. Do Right:

DWF, 33 Full-figured Italian red headed non-smoker seeks SBM 30-35 non-smoker with sense of humor, must love jazz, sports, and romantic movies.

The next day as Francesca turned in her ad, she wondered what kind of desperate men might apply. She was given a phone number and pic code by the clerk. There was a twenty-four-hour delay to set-up a voice message for prospective dates. This was a safe way to keep her anonymity until she was ready to pick the right escort. Francesca decided to wait several days before checking her responses.

On Thursday she finally began to listen to her messages. She heard the first three, she cringed when they started with a greeting of babe or honey, and she quickly learned the value of the delete option. The fourth candidate's deep sexy soulful voice caught her curiosity. She listened to his message attentively, "Good Evening, I've never answered one of these ads but thought I would take a chance. My name is Damien, and I'm 33 years old. I enjoy sports, Sleepless in Seattle, and I play the saxophone. Please call me and let's talk."

Francesca was impressed with the reference to the romantic movie and loved the sound of a sax. She decided this one might be worth contacting.

After several days of rehearsing her conversation, she finally got the nerve to call Damien. Several rings went by before she got a response.

"Hello," he responded in the voice that had mesmerized her earlier.

"May I please speak with Damien?" she said in a business-like manner.

"This is Damien. How may I help you?"

"This is Francesca. You answered my ad in the Personals."

"I'm glad you called. I hope my message didn't sound too formal, but I was nervous recording it. This is the first time I've ever done this sort of thing."

"This is also my first time dealing with an ad. I'm glad I wasn't the only nervous person." Francesca's voice became less tense as she empathized this new experience for both of them.

"Would you like to get together for lunch? I'm taking a vacation day from work tomorrow and would have some free time." Damien replied.

Francesca didn't want to accept this quick of an offer to meet but his soothing voice seemed to relax her, "That would be fine. Where would you like to meet?"

"Are you familiar with the Cumberland Mall area?" he asked.

"Yes."

"Is the Segreto Notte all right with you?"

She quickly responded, "Yes, that would be great!" Damien's choice of a restaurant impressed her.

10

"Let's meet a few minutes before noon in order to avoid the lunch crowd."

"That sounds good to me but how do I recognize you?" Francesca anxiously awaited his response.

"I'll be holding a yellow rose. What will you be wearing?"

"I'll be in a purple dress."

"I look forward to meeting you," Damien responded in an inviting manner.

"I look forward to meeting you, too."

Both of them hung up the phone at the same time. Francesca thought the gesture of a yellow rose showed originality and wasn't too pushy since yellow represented friendship. She went to her closet to examine her dress and wondered if it would be appropriate for a March day. She then chose a pair of semi-dress heels and completed the ensemble with simple gold stud and a matching gold rope necklace. Francesca glanced at the clock when she saw it was eleven and decided to go to bed.

The next day, finally her staff meeting was done. As she rushed towards the elevator, she informed the receptionist she wouldn't be back until late afternoon due to a meeting with a client off grounds. Francesca ran to her car and exited the parking garage onto Peachtree Street near 14th Street. Her office at Colony Square was a great location since it was a few minutes away from her place. As she merged onto I-75 northbound from Midtown, she prayed traffic wouldn't be congested. Luckily, it was smooth driving until she turned onto the loop for the Perimeter Parkway, a stalled vehicle blocked a lane. Traffic cleared eventually to make a right turn at the end of the exit ramp onto Cobb Parkway. It seemed like time was in slow motion while she was waiting for the light at Cumberland Parkway to change. It was almost noon as she drove up the hill into the Segreto Notte's parking lot on the right. Francesca gave a quick glance in the rearview mirror. She retouched her lipstick and fluffed her hair then exited her car.

As Francesca entered the building, she scanned the lobby for the man with the yellow rose but didn't see him. She went to the hostess stand and checked in to see if the party of "Damien" was already there. The hostess informed her he had not arrived yet. Francesca sat down in an elegant high-back armchair as she waited for her guest. Her eyes kept going towards the door when heard the hostess greet new customers. Several minutes later her waiting had ended as a gentleman entered carrying a yellow rose. She noticed he stood still as his eyes scanned the lobby. Suddenly, their eyes met and for that moment time ceased to exist. Francesca felt her heart pounding profusely as he began his approach towards her.

He stood in front of her and called her name "Francesca?" His lustrous voice made her pause as she tried to enunciate the words to correctly respond to his question. She had to clear her throat before she could speak.

"My name is Francesca Stefani." She stood up and extended her hand. Instead of shaking her hand, he held her hand and leaned down to kiss it before he gave the yellow rose.

"My name is Damien Sommers, it is nice to meet you," he said displaying a faint smile. Francesca couldn't help but notice him wearing a pair of Khaki pants and Armani shirt with the top button opened, which gave him a sophisticated appearance. Damien was six three, had a creamy mocha complexion, brown eyes, short curly black hair, and a light mustache. His facial hair continued a patch below his lip along with a border of it along his lower jaw line. It was apparent he worked out on a regular basis.

13

"It is nice to meet you, too!" As she completed her statement the hostess announced that their table was ready. When they approached the table, Damien pulled out the chair for her. She sat down and thought she was glad she had chosen these heels since she would have been nine inches shorter than him in flats. After ordering the meal it was time for the real conversation. Before Francesca had the chance to ask the typical background questions Damien began with the obvious one.

"What do you do for a living and how long have you lived in Atlanta?" he asked.

She was relieved not to be the first one to initiate the questioning. "I have been in Atlanta for four years. I have been working on my clinical shifts towards my B.A. Psychology Degree from Georgia State University. I have supported myself by working for a Midtown P/R firm. And you?" Francesca's self-assuredness hid her nervousness.

Damien responded, "My job transferred me several months ago to Atlanta from Charleston. I have been employed by a national company in a management position. What do you do during your free time?"

"I really haven't had much free time, but I love jazz music especially Oleta Adams, watching movies, and outdoor activities since I live near Piedmont Park. How often do you play the sax?" Francesca asked inquisitively.

"Whenever I get a chance, but I haven't performed in any clubs lately. I worked long hours some weeks since I had to entertain clients after regular office hours. Your time for lunch is limited today. Correct? I would like to see you again. May I have your number?" Damien asked as he stared into her eyes.

Francesca felt at ease with Damien and was attracted to him. He didn't appear to have any bizarre habits during the meal and only fidgeted with his right ring finger a few times which had a gold band with a diamond in the center of it.

"That would be nice," she wrote down her number and handed it to him. When the check came, she reached for her purse to pay but Damien took it. He placed his American Express Gold card on the tray. She felt awkward when he paid but it had been a while since she had been treated to a meal. Damien stood up and pulled out the chair for Francesca while he reminded her not to forget her rose. He then escorted her out of the restaurant to her car. As they approached her white 1970 Mustang, she asked where he had parked his car. Damien pointed at a new white 1994 Lexus with tinted windows. She couldn't help but be awed. Francesca unlocked her car and turned around to say goodbye. "It was a pleasure meeting you and thank you for the rose. I look forward to seeing you again."

"The pleasure was all mine. I'll call you in a couple of days to set-up our next date. Have a nice rest of your day," he gently took her hand and gave it a final goodbye kiss.

Francesca felt chills through her whole body and could smell the fresh scent of his cologne on her hand. She knew it would be hard to concentrate on anything-else the rest of the day. Francesca looked at her watch and knew she needed to leave for her client meeting. However, she couldn't help herself as she took one last glance at Damien as his near perfect body walked to his car.

CHAPTER
THREE

Screams of pain were heard, Dr. Kent, a third-year resident was running up Level 2. Shadows from the sunset crisscrossed Francesca's bloody and motionless body. Dr. Kent rushed around the corner to be at her side. He put on his gloves from his pocket then started his Primary Survey of her vitals. He found her non-responsive, airway was compromised, respiratory rate elevated, and pulse rate rapid. He heard footsteps from the parking ramp, he called for help. Two first-year interns appeared. He instructed one to hold her head in C-Spine position and the other one assisted him when they slowly turned her body from the side to back. Dr. Kent saw the reason for the compromised breathing. It was apparent her nose was fractured from the swelling and bruising around her nose along with under her eyes. The right side of her face was sunken it confirmed Dr. Kent's fears, she had a maxillofacial trauma.

He couldn't help but see the pool of blood from her leg. As he applied pressure to stop the blood, a security guard appeared stating he had notified the hospital via radio. Soon the sound of the ambulance's siren could be heard inside the parking garage. Dr. Kent turned his head as the medics rushed from the ambulance. A bag-valve-mask was put gently over her face to regulate her breathing. Francesca's blood pressure was decreasing, and her skin was cool even though she was wearing long sleeves. Bandages were being applied to her leg which appeared to control the bleeding. A medic applied a C-collar. The intern released his position. The men rolled the body onto her side to complete the Secondary Survey. She was placed onto the back board. Dr. Kent had noticed a large bruise on her back. They lifted the backboard to a stretcher and elevated her feet. They loaded Francesca into the ambulance. An IV of Ringer's had been started. It was apparent to Dr. Kent that Francesca was experiencing shock.

Within five minutes they were in the trauma area of the emergency room. The C-collar was removed after confirmation of no apparent spinal injury. Dr. Kent reassessed the leg laceration which didn't appear to have additional bleeding. However, he was concerned with possible internal bleeding due to the bruise on her back and facial injuries. He needed to assess the specific type of shock and ordered a CT scan. Dr. Kent received the results as her blood pressure was bottoming out. He immediately arranged for the surgeon on-call to prep for her arrival to the operating room. His suspicions were confirmed, she was suffering from hemorrhagic shock. Dr. Kent released treatment of Francesca to the surgeon.

He returned to the ER to finish his paperwork. He asked the nurse if she had found ID or had a file on his patient. Dr. Kent was inspecting her ID. He discovered his patient's name was Francesca Stefani and she was completing her clinical rotations with the psychology department. The nurse had made notations that she was unable to reach the first emergency contact. Dr. Kent dialed the number for Damien Sommers.

The phone rang numerous times before a male voice from the answering machine was heard. Dr. Kent began his message, "This is Dr. Kent from Georgia Baptist Hospital on behalf of Francesca Stefani. Please call 555-1994." As he finished his call, he noticed the fresh blood stains on his scrubs. Before he found Francesca in the garage, he had been exhausted from working sixteen hours and looking forward to a good night's sleep. He was full of adrenalin and knew he would be unable to sleep if he went home. Dr. Kent instructed the nurse he was going to the staff quarters to take a shower then he would be checking on Ms.

Stefani's surgery. He wanted to be paged when Mr. Sommers returned his call.

Several hours passed and it was almost 11 pm before Dr. Kent received the page he was expecting. He dialed the operator and waited for the connection to the caller.

"Hello, this is Dr. Kent."

"Dr. Kent my name is Damien Sommers. I'm returning your call about Francesca Stefani."

"Mr. Sommers, I'm sorry to inform you that Ms. Stefani has been involved in an accident." Dr. Kent was attempting to speak calmly.

"How did it happen?" Damien asked in a business-like manner.

"She was found unconscious in the hospital parking garage." Dr. Kent continued to inform him of the situation.

"What is her condition?"

"She is in surgery. I would prefer to give more details when you get here. Just page me from the front desk. How soon can you be here?" Dr. Kent felt Mr. Sommers wasn't grasping the possible seriousness of her injuries.

"Give me thirty minutes. Thank you, Dr. Kent." The tone in Damien's voice never changed.

Dr. Kent was puzzled by Mr. Sommers' reaction that had seemed extremely calm for the circumstances. Although he wasn't privy to the relationship with Ms. Stefani, he thought there should have been more urgency in the man's voice. Dr. Kent realized that the man was probably in shock from the news.

CHAPTER FOUR

Damien had kept his promise and called Francesca within a few days. They had decided to meet on Saturday night. She took the initiative and invited him to her place for an Italian dinner. During the week Francesca had several phone conversations that involved Angie's dating advice for her dinner including wardrobe and perfume.

On Saturday morning, the phone rang awoken Francesca from a deep sleep. It was Julie Peters with an invitation to the zoo with her five-year-old nieces. Julie was a slender twenty-five-year-old black woman who was a computer programmer. She was married for the past three years to Ron Peters an attractive twenty-six-year-old black computer executive who always had a well-polished appearance. They had become friends thru Brian when Francesca first moved to Atlanta. The tone of Julie's voice sounded like she could use adult companionship on this adventure in babysitting. Francesca agreed to meet at eleven but reminded Julie she had prep work to do for her date.

She arrived at the zoo and spotted Julie. The temperature was unusually hot for March. "Hi everyone." Francesca greeted the group.

"So, tell me all about him," Julie exchanged a hug.

"Damien is my age, an executive, and definitely not bad on the eyes. He plays the sax." Her eyes lit up.

"The sax music always gets you in trouble."

"We only had lunch. I'm excited for this new experience. Who knew I would be excited over an ad?" Francesca laughed.

"I was surprised. I thought you would have reconnected with Kenny. You did say you loved his tanned well-toned body," Julie smiled.

"Kenny was too young for me. A ten-year difference made me nervous. Kenny needed to stay in the friend zone. Although, I have enjoyed the company of tall men."

24

"Be careful."

"Okay. That's enough about the love life."

Francesca enjoyed herself with Julie's group, but the sun beat down and exhausted her. It was already three in the afternoon. Julie and the girls said goodbye as Francesca left the zoo.

It was five-thirty when she put the final touches on the salad and turned down the oven for the baked ziti. She had finished dressing into her sleeveless blue dress. She quickly sprayed on her favorite Passion perfume and put on her last earring as she heard the doorbell ring. Francesca fluffed her shoulder length red hair when she opened the door. Damien was dressed casually and presented a bouquet of yellow roses. He kissed her hand and followed her to the sofa.

"Thank you for the lovely flowers. Let me put these in water. Can I get you a glass of red wine while I'm in the kitchen?" She asked attempting to be a good hostess.

"Thank you that would be great." Damien responded, paused then continued, "I really like your place."

She returned with two glasses of wine, "Would you like to see the rest of my place?" As Francesca looked for Dizzy but realized he had disappeared.

He nodded yes and followed her down the hallway as she showed him framed photographs she had taken along the East coast. He complimented her photography skills as they went back to the dining area. Then she opened the French style doors and entered the fenced in patio. They sat at the white iron table surrounded by four matching chairs with beige cushions.

"I've always liked Victorian style houses. Do you spend much time out here?" he asked inquisitively.

"Whenever I get the chance. I'm more relaxed out here," Francesca answered attentively.

The oven timer buzzed for the garlic bread and Francesca excused herself to go to the kitchen. A few minutes later she returned to the patio and invited Damien to the dining room table. It was set with matching china on red woven placements with the vase of flowers as a centerpiece. She served the meal and poured another glass of wine for both of them.

26

She wanted more information about him but didn't want to seem too pushy. After some hesitation, she took a deep breath, "I hope this is enough for you. I wasn't sure how much to cook."

"It's fine, everything tasted great. This is a great neighborhood across from the park," he responded with a faint smile.

"I love this area but I'm not sure if I'll stay in Atlanta after school is done. Does your job keep you in this area for a while?" Francesca then realized she might have asked for too many details for a second date.

"I'm not sure. I lived in Charleston for several years before my job moved me here. I didn't like Charleston when I first moved there but at the end, I really grew to love it!" Damien answered enthusiastically.

"Are you from Charleston?" she asked calmly.

"No, I'm from upstate Georgia where I went to school for my master's degree. Some of my family still lives in that area. It is nice being in Atlanta since I can visit with them over the weekends."

"How many brothers and sisters are in your family?" she waited anxiously for his response.

"I'm the middle son and have four sisters. My mother died of cancer when I was young, but my dad lives upstate and resides on the bench as a judge. My brothers are both lawyers. We are extremely close and try to see each other as much as possible. What about your family?" Damien had shown a degree of sadness when he mentioned his mother.

"I have two brothers who live out of state. My parents live a few hours from here near the mountains. My mother is a retired teacher, but my father works as Director of Cardiology. We see each other every couple of months."

"If I'm not being too nosey, why did you place a Personal ad?" he curiously asked.

"After a few years of a bad marriage, I got a divorce. I haven't been in a relationship for quite a while and with my schedule, I felt this would be the safest way to meet someone. Why did you answer the ad?" Francesca wasn't sure of his response or if she would like it.

28

"I wanted to have a social life but didn't want to mix it with my business life. I lived with a woman named Tina and her boys before moving here." He stated in a casual manner.

"Would you like to sit on the sofa for coffee?" Francesca was pondering his last response mentioning another woman. Either Damien still loves her, or he was extremely honest about his past.

"Yes, thank you," Damien said.

After moving to the living room, she handed the coffee cup and saucer to Damien. Francesca turned on the stereo to her favorite jazz musician and sat down next to him. She felt an easiness with him as they laughed and talked for the next several hours. The chime of the grandfather clock interrupted their conversation as they noticed it was eleven. Damien had a surprised look on his face.

"It's late and I need to get a good night's sleep since I'm to visit my dad tomorrow. Thank you for a lovely evening," he apprehensively replied.

They stood up and he followed Francesca to the door. She turned around to face him.

"I'm glad you accepted my invitation. I had a wonderful time tonight." Francesca responded.

Damien leaned towards Francesca giving her a gentle kiss on the cheek and a brief hug. The door was opened. Damien stood in the doorway and turned back towards Francesca. They gazed into each other's eyes as he was moved closer to her. Suddenly he stopped inches before her face, "It's late, I really should go. I'll call you later this week." Damien walked down the front steps to his car. He looked back at her and waved goodbye.

Francesca responded with a wave and closed the door. She felt the evening had gone well but couldn't understand the abrupt end. It puzzled her why Damien kept moving closer on the sofa, hugged her, and then rejected the idea of kissing on the lips. Maybe he was old fashioned, or he wasn't sure of a positive reaction. There was no way to predict it would have been such an innocent evening. Disappointed, Francesca cleaned up the kitchen and went to bed.

The sound of thunder awakened Francesca from her sleep during the early morning hours. After she put on her robe, she peered through the curtains to the courtyard while holding Dizzy. The sky was dark, and the rain drizzled down her window pane.

Dizzy jumped from her hold. Francesca opened the front door to get the Sunday paper. She sat on the sofa sipping her coffee and read the paper when the phone rang. It was Angie's mother stating Angie had been in a car accident and was in surgery. Francesca said she would drive up there as soon as possible.

The conversation ended; she felt the need to call Brian Chambers. He was part of her main inner circle.

Brian was like a brother to her. Since he had a brief affair with Angie, she knew he would want to be informed. She had admired Brian's determination in overcoming obstacles to achieve his success. He had lost his father at a young age in a car accident. Luckily, due to the wrongful death lawsuit from the drunk driver, he had money to complete college. Brian had an active life being a member of Omega Psi Phi while attending Morehouse College earning his Political Science B.A. Degree. He then acquired his J.D. Degree at Emory University School of Law. He was an attorney working in corporate law for a prestigious firm near Peachtree Center. She was able to contact Brian, he accepted her request to accompany her on the trip. She was glad he said yes considering his busy schedule which included teaching karate to "at-risk" youth.

31

Francesca remembered she had to contact her boss to inform him of the situation. Her boss understood and told her he would clear her schedule for the next few days. She then called Julie to take care of Dizzy since she already had a key to her place. Francesca quickly threw some things into an overnight bag and raced down the walkway to her car.

She drove past Piedmont Hospital on Peachtree Road NE to Buckhead. Soon she made the left turn down the steep hill to "The Piedmont" on Colonial Home Drive. As she went around the curve past the back of the five-story luxury building, she then stopped at the front entrance. A six-foot, twenty-six-year-old attractive black man with a muscular build was standing outside at the smoked glass door with the elegant wrought iron framing it. Brian's place was a tranquil location with the wooded park surrounding it in this exclusive neighborhood. Francesca stepped out of her car and opened the trunk. He gave her a hug then closed the trunk after he dropped his bag in it. The two entered the car and drove away towards I-75 northbound to see Angie. They hoped the news would be good when they arrived at their final destination.

CHAPTER
FIVE

Damien waited for the gates of The Pointe before he headed towards the Perimeter Parkway. Within moments he was on I-20 eastbound going to Midtown. He needed to find out her condition and who had been contacted. Apparently, she hadn't informed Brian of the threats since she was found alone. Damien entered the hospital garage and searched for a parking spot. He exited the car and headed for the stairwell on Level 2, but the police caution tape stopped him. His queasy body shook at the sight from the pool of blood that covered the pavement. Many emotions went through Damien's mind as the realization that it belonged to Francesca and he should have stopped it. As someone who prided himself on his rigid self-control, he found it difficult to keep his emotions in balance.

He headed down Level 1 to the hospital entrance. Upon entering the lobby, Damien found his composure and requested for Dr. Kent to be paged. The doctor appeared and introduced himself to Damien. The two were taking the elevator to the I.C.U. on the 2 Tower. Dr. Kent explained Francesca's condition to Damien.

"Mr. Sommers, she had internal bleeding from blunt force trauma in her lower back. Her breathing was compromised due to a fractured nose and cheekbone. The procedure resolved the zygoma which involved insertion of thin hardware through small incisions in her mouth. This assisted her cheekbone stabilization. In addition, she suffered a laceration on her leg and fractured her left ankle. Ms. Stefani went into a coma."

"I thought you said her conditions was stable. Why is she in a coma?" Damien inquired.

"She went into shock due to the bleeding. According to her CT scan there weren't any blood clots near the brain. Everyone recovers at different rates after surgery and this kind of shock to the system. It could take one hour or several days for her to wake up." Dr. Kent attempted to explain.

"Would she be able to remember the incident? Who has been notified of her condition?" Damien asked calmly.

Dr. Kent informed him, "We have to wait until she wakes up. Her memory of the incident might be gradual or sudden. We don't want to traumatize her any further so it would be best for her to remember on her own. You are the only one I was able to contact."

Damien's tone never changed as he asked, "I can make the appropriate contacts. Can I see her?"

"Here is her area. You can stay for a few minutes at first but would have to leave while the staff checks her condition. There is a waiting area down the hall. The nurse will find you when you can return. I'll be back in the morning. If you need anything just inform the nurse. Goodnight."

"Goodnight, Dr. Kent." Damien extended his hand.

Damien stood by Francesca's bedside, starred at her I.V. His expression changed from one of control to sorrow for her broken face and tortured body. He reached for her hand to hold it tightly, maybe she would feel his presence and wake-up. There was no response from her. Damien spoke in a soft voice.

"I'm sorry this happened to you. I could have stopped this. It's entirely my fault!"

35

"Excuse me sir, you'll have to leave for about thirty minutes while the I.V. gets changed. I'll get you from the waiting room."

Damien left Francesca and entered the waiting room. Damien made the decision this would be the best time to contact Brian. He picked up the phone in the waiting area and dialed his number.

"Hello," Brian answered.

"Brian, this is Damien. Francesca has been hurt and is in the I.C.U. at Georgia Baptist."

"What happened?" Brian abruptly asked.

"She fell down the parking garage stairs after she finished her shift."

"Have you called Julie and Ron yet? What about her father, Dr. Stefani?" Brian was anxious to find out if Damien had notified the others.

"No, you're the only one I have contacted," Damien replied.

"Don't worry, I'll make the rest of the calls," Brian assured him.

"Thank you. I'll see you in a while. Just come to the I.C.U. area."

"I'll see you within the hour. Goodbye."

"Goodbye." Damien responded.

Damien tried to relax while sitting in the waiting room mindlessly looking at the television. He then kept looking at his watch and couldn't help but notice that thirty minutes had already passed. He heard voices from the doorway. Damien stood up and greeted Brian, Julie, and Ron. He informed them of Francesca's condition and was waiting on the nurse to notify him when she could have visitors again. Suddenly, the I.C.U. nurse appeared with a solemn look on her face.

"Mr. Sommers, please follow me. The doctor needs to speak with you."

37

CHAPTER
SIX

Several days had passed since Francesca and Brian had received the news of Angie's accident. Upon their arrival to the hospital, they were informed surgery had been performed for a ruptured spleen. Unfortunately, Angie's spleen had to be removed but a complete recovery was expected. After several days of hospital visits, Angie insisted that Francesca and Brian return to their lives in Atlanta. Angie said her sister had offered to take care of her and her ex-husband would take the children while she recuperated. Francesca was hesitant but felt things were under control. They said their goodbyes as Francesca and Brian returned to Atlanta with the promise from Angie she would call if she needed anything from them.

Francesca returned to her place once Brian was dropped off. Dizzy greeted her warmly. She then listened to her answering machine as she unpacked her bag. Her face became ecstatic when she heard Damien's voice. She immediately called him back and explained her recent trip to be with an injured friend. He expressed his sympathy about the ordeal and offered to take her out for coffee for a change of pace. Francesca declined since she was exhausted from the events of the past few days. They made plans to see each other over the weekend. After her conversation with Damien, she prepared her clothes for the next day of work and fell into a deep sleep with Dizzy by her side.

Thursday was a busy day for Francesca at work since she had to reschedule several clients' appointments and got caught up on events of the staff meeting she had missed. It was six when she left the office. She had arrived at her place and was getting ready for a shower when she heard the phone ringing. To her surprise it was Damien with an offer of pizza and a video at her place. Francesca was surprised by the offer since it wasn't the weekend yet. She accepted it then frantically hopped in and out of the shower. As she dried off, she ran to her closet and grabbed her blue jean skirt with matching peasant blouse. The doorbell rang as she put one more dab of perfume behind her ear. She opened the door and offered to help carry the food, but Damien declined. He proceeded to the dining room table to set down the items as she returned from the kitchen with plates and wine glasses. They brought their fixed plates and drinks to the coffee table in the living room. Damien gave Francesca a video of "Sleepless in Seattle," which he had rented, then she happily inserted it into the VCR. She returned next to him on the sofa. Over the next couple of hours, the two enjoyed the romantic movie and dinner together.

It was around nine by the time the movie was over. Francesca turned off the television and popped her favorite Oleta Adams tape in the stereo. She returned to the sofa with Damien. He moved extremely close to her. She was glad for the closeness but remembered his cautious reactions at the end of their last date. Francesca felt the urge to investigate if he would pull back again.

"Thank you for the movie and dinner. I was surprised to hear from you since it wasn't the weekend."

"I knew you had several days of chaos and work would probably be hectic for you. I thought you might enjoy a night of take-out and a mellow movie," Damien attentively responded.

"That was extremely thoughtful of you. I really needed this to break the tension I have experienced," Francesca replied in a stressed tone.

Don't Judge A Book

"I'm glad it helped. If you're still tense, I've been told I give a great massage. Would you like one?" Damien asked.

Francesca was shocked at the question, but it definitely answered her curiosity about his intentions towards her. "Actually, that sounds like a great idea." Francesca walked to the other room. She returned from her bedroom with a comforter and he had moved the coffee table to the side of the sofa. Francesca was slightly nervous as she sat down next to Damien on the comforter. He then motioned for her to lie down on her stomach. Damien blew on his hands to warm them from the cold wine glass. He performed skillfully, as he gently massaged her shoulders and neck with his warm masculine hands. Damien slowly kissed the back of her neck and began nibbling her earlobes. Francesca was spellbound by his relaxation techniques. She felt the compulsion to inform Damien there had been a lapse in her love life but choose to express it in a casual manner in case she misunderstood his actions.

"Damien, it's been so long since I've been with a guy that an ankle excites me."

"The wind pretty much does it for me!" He replied dryly.

Francesca's future intimacy with Damien had been confirmed. Damien turned over Francesca's body to her back as he continued to massage her. His hands tenderly caressed when he slid them slowly under her blouse and found the proof of her desire. She removed her blouse as he removed his shirt. Damien and Francesca embraced in a long passionate kiss as their movements had left their bare bodies wrapped in the comforter. The touch of Francesca's delicate fingers through his curly hair then across his spine, she felt increased his desire as he breathed heavier with each thrust of his body that penetrated her. Damien's actions had enthralled in her cries of ecstasy. Francesca felt heights of passion that hadn't been reached in a while. Their lovemaking left them oblivious to their surroundings as the tape had auto rewound for the second time. Their bodies were glistening with a mixture of his cologne and her perfume as Damien gently kissed Francesca on the forehead as she laid on his chest. She was mesmerized by a state of elated bliss.

"Francesca, this isn't just a one-night stand."

"That makes me feel better. I was nervous being intimate with you and what your impression would be if I had made the first move. Dating was so much different for us in the 1970's. Back then we were lucky to know our partner's first names, forget knowing their last names!"

"Hello, my name is Damien Sommers, nice to meet you!"

Damien's sarcastic sense of humor made her laugh. His comments had revived her optimism in men. She felt this wasn't going to be another illicit relationship and he was worthy of sincerity. Unfortunately, they both had to work in the morning, and it was the middle of the night. Damien informed her that he felt it would be best if he went home since he hadn't brought a change of clothes for work and they both needed sleep. Francesca put on her robe as he dressed and escorted him to the door. Damien embraced Francesca and kissed her proving his current desire. He then said good night and promised to phone her when she returned home from work.

It was hard for Francesca to concentrate at work as she thought about the events of the past evening. She had another couple of hours of prep work to complete for her presentation to a new client. One of her co-workers had invited her out for drinks but she had declined. It was quitting time on Friday. Francesca looked forward to getting home to shower and catch up on the sleep she had missed the past week. After she fed Dizzy, who had been in hiding whenever Damien appeared, she then showered. Francesca fell asleep and had been napping when she was awakened by the phone. Just as he had promised, it was Damien. He had just arrived home from work but invited her to his place for a late dinner. Although she had been tired, the nap had revitalized her. She thought since it was the weekend, she could always sleep late over the next two days. Francesca accepted his invitation. He gave her directions to his place via I-75 after he asked about her comfort zone with Cobb County.

Damien suggested she should bring changes of clothing for the weekend. He then explained he lived in a high security gated community and the guard would have to call him from the gatehouse to be buzzed into the gates. Francesca hung up the phone. Frantically, she looked in her closet for the most alluring lingerie and daytime attire. Her toiletries were packed including perfume, she filled the food and water bowls for Dizzy. Francesca went out her front door to her car and drove off northbound towards Damien's place. On the way, she stopped to pick up a bottle of red wine for the occasion. It took her about twenty-five minutes to the gatehouse of The Pointe. Francesca was impressed with the grounds and the elegant clubhouse with an adjacent swimming pool and tennis courts. She informed the guard of Damien's name. The gates opened and the guard directed her up the hill to make the right turn to get to Mr. Sommers' townhouse.

Francesca parked her car in front of his townhouse and took her overnight bag as she exited her car. He was waiting in the archway before she had a chance to enter the home. Damien greeted Francesca then escorted her into his place and promptly closed the door. She put down her bag by the sofa and offered to assist him with the meal while he took the bottle of wine. He thanked her for the wine and declined her help. He told her it was his turn to serve her. Damien had jazz music that played in the background while he was in the kitchen. He prepared the finishing touches on the filet mignon and mushroom with wine sauce. She was startled as she heard a voice saying, "The phone is ringing, the phone is ringing!" Damien ran upstairs and answered the phone.

Damien returned from a bedroom and invited Francesca to an elegantly set dining room table complete with candles. Due to the atmosphere, she was glad she hadn't dressed in jeans but instead had worn a dress. She complimented him on his cooking skills and his taste for interior decorating with the room filled with framed landscapes along with high end furniture. They glanced into each other's eyes through the flickering lights of the candles during the dinner. Their desire became evident as Damien reached for her hand as he stood from the table, he guided her to stand into his warm embrace and passionate kisses.

CHAPTER SEVEN

Francesca's surgeon, Dr. Stevens and her hospital supervisor, Dr. Barber introduced themselves to Damien. Dr. Barber stated she was conscious but wasn't sure how long she would be awake. Dr. Stevens then informed Damien that it wasn't an accident and the police had found a tire iron at the top of the stairwell. It had been used to hit Ms. Stefani's back and forced her to plunge down the stairs. He continued to state Francesca's recovery would probably be the next four to six weeks. She would need a liquid or soft diet until her sutures dissolved and the hardware in her mouth has stabilized. The first couple of weeks she would need to have her head propped up to breathe properly. Her medications would consist of antibiotics and mild pain relievers. She should be able to walk without the cast in about four to six weeks but would still need a cane for a while. Damien quickly was walking to Francesca's bed as Dr. Stevens pulled the curtain shut to give the two of them privacy. As he was bending down to give her a gentle kiss on the lips, she was moving her head slightly and instead he touched her uninjured cheek. Damien attempted to hold her hand, but she jerked it back, "Damien, what are you doing here?"

"The hospital called since I was your emergency contact and informed me of your condition. I was worried and thought I should be here for you. How are you feeling?" Damien tried to look into her eyes, but she looked away.

"I feel like I've been tackled by the Carolina Panthers, but I'll survive. Has my dad been contacted?" Francesca responded coldly.

"Yes, I called Brian who offered to call Dr. Stefani. Brian is in the waiting room with Julie and Ron down the hallway. Is there anything I can do for you such as notify your boss or check on your place over the next few days?" Damien appeared to show compassion.

"No, I'd feel more comfortable if Brian would take care of those things. I don't want to take up anymore of your time. Thank you for coming to check on me and I'll make sure that I change the emergency contact person." Francesca retained her defiant tone.

"I wish you would accept my offer since assistance is needed for the next several weeks. I'm sorry this happened to you, I should have protected you after the threats were made!" Damien stressed his objections to her demands.

"In the future, I'll try to be more cautious. Don't worry, I won't be your problem anymore. I'm sure you are probably tired and need to get sleep for work. Once again thank you for coming. If you don't mind, please send in Brian and my other friends to see me on your way out. Goodbye Damien!"

"I hope you feel better soon. I'll send the others to you. Take care of yourself. Goodbye Francesca."

As per her demands, Damien returned to the waiting room and informed Brian he would be able to visit her. Brian had a puzzling look on his face as Damien started to walk towards the elevator.

"Aren't you staying to visit her more? We are only staying for a short time. You can visit more with her."

"Brian, she doesn't want to have anything to do with me. I offered to help her, but she told me that she would no longer be my problem anymore. I guess I shouldn't be surprised after my statements to her last week."

"I'll talk to her and tell her it's alright to accept your offer. I have to be out of town for about a week and your help is needed. I understand she is hurt by the situation between the two of you, but I'll see what I can do for you." Brian hopes to ease the tension of the situation.

"I'm going to give her some time to calm down. She doesn't need any more stress tonight. I'll give you a call later." Damien's response shown his composure stable again.

Damien said his goodbyes to Brian, Julie, and Ron. He was emotionally drained after his ordeal with Francesca's condition and her reaction towards him. Damien still cared about her but due to his past circumstances he thought he needed to have distance from her. He hoped Brian would be able to diffuse the negative feelings she was experiencing. Damien looked at the time when he arrived at The Pointe. He realized it was three in the morning and had to decide if he would try to sleep or take a shower. He stretched out on the sofa and turned on the television within minutes his eyes were closing. The alarm rang making Damien jump from the sofa. He ran into the shower to prepare for work. Exhaustion was felt from the events of the night. Later that day after work, the voice of the phone startled Damien from a deep sleep. The caller was Brian. He updated the results of his conversation with Francesca.

"She said that she didn't accept your offer since she was trying to abide by your recent request. I was finally able to convince her it would be in her best interest to accept your offer."

"Thank you. It is only a temporary solution, but I think it would help with her recovery. I'm going to change my clothes and go to the hospital to visit her," Damien graciously responded.

"I promise you she should be more receptive towards you tonight. I have just left the hospital, so I won't be returning until tomorrow. I'm making arrangements to pick-up her car once the Atlanta Police Department has completed their investigation. Thank you for still wanting to help." Brian's intervention should assist with Francesca's recovery.

"I'll talk to you soon. Goodnight Brian."

Later that night Damien arrived at the hospital and saw a smile on Francesca's face when she saw him.

"I'm glad you came back," Francesca motioned for him to come closer.

"I understand you were upset earlier. That wasn't my intention," he patted her hand.

"Brian told me you wanted to help. Don't worry I plan to be self-sufficient as soon as possible for you to return to your normal routine." She made her intentions clear.

"Don't be concerned about my situation. The main issue is your health. After I check my schedule, I would cover certain shifts after coordination with Brian," Damien insisted.

"Thank you. I'm really tired. If you wouldn't mind, I need to rest." She loved his compassion and hated to send him away.

"Tomorrow details can be finalized. Get rest." Damien bent over to kiss her hand before he left.

Francesca could hold back the tears no more after Damien exited her area. The emotions she felt overwhelmed her. Francesca couldn't figure out if it was sympathy or genuine feelings of love, he had for her. Francesca had to keep herself guarded and not show her true emotions in order not to get hurt by him again.

It was another night of restless sleep. The trauma of the attack brought flashbacks of the darkness of her childhood. Francesca was dreaming of his clammy hands that touched her body while pushing her back onto the ground. His lips attempted to kiss her with the stink of his bad breath. She was trying to push him off and scream but knew it would never be heard. Finally, when he was satisfied, he left her. Francesca woke up in a cold sweat. She had to pray this was only a nightmare but soon realized it had been her life. During her late elementary school years her male teenager babysitter had abused her for years. She had lived with this secret her whole life. Francesca was feeling the need to be strong and not inform Damien about the flashbacks. She didn't want pity from him.

CHAPTER EIGHT

Damien enjoyed the comfort of his custom-made sofa as he watched sports while Francesca's head was laid on his lap. The rain gently beat on the window when their Sunday afternoon plans to go to Piedmont Park had been cancelled. Francesca had decided during her recent trip upstate to have the weekend off from her hospital shift due to the possibility of traveling back to see Angie. It was past noon, but Francesca only wore Damien's Panther jersey scented with Cool Water cologne and he had thrown on a pair of white terry cloth shorts. She felt she had known him all her life. The past several days they had been inseparable and shared the details of their past lives. Damien had opened up about his relationship in Charleston with Tina Perez, who was widowed with two boys. He stated during his last encounter with Tina she wanted him to move back. Francesca was a little nervous by that comment. She assumed since he was living in Atlanta and he was being intimate with her, she decided not to worry about Mrs. Perez. Francesca opened up about her relationship with her ex-husband, Tom.

She stated Tom married her after a whirlwind romance. "In the beginning the marriage was calm until I started working two jobs to help with the bills and pay for the advancement of Tom's education. We had the appearance of a perfect couple. Tom was an attentive husband at first. Even though, I still kept a neat place, did his laundry, and prepared all his meals in advance he would go into violent tantrums. Once Tom earned his MBA degree and became a district manager, I thought life would be easier. I was wrong! Tom's behavior became more disturbing with the verbal abuse and broken items that had been thrown. I coped by going through a drinking phase to numb me. The last straw was him buying a sports car without telling me and finding love letters in our bill drawer from his secretary, Maria! When I confronted Tom, he told me if I had spent more time at home instead of working, he wouldn't have done those things or had affairs. I promptly stopped drinking and left him." Francesca looked drained.

"Do you want to continue?" Damien gave a hug.

"That's it for my marriage. My last relationship was with Kenny Underwood, a twenty-four-year-old Morehouse College medical student. Brian was his "Big Brother" for Omega Psi Phi, which is where I met Kenny." Francesca paused a moment when she recalled memories of the fraternity's STEP competitions and the excitement she felt with him. "I decided due to the age difference to be just friends." She looked at Damien as he listened closely to the stories of her past which included the drinking problem. They were both silent.

After an hour, Damien's game had ended, and he became restless as his channel surfing was unable to find a favorable program. He used the remote to switch from the television to listen to smooth jazz music on the stereo. Damien noticed that Francesca had fallen back to sleep in his lap. The rhythm of the pounding rain on the window had put Damien in an amorous mood.

He took a partially melted ice cube from his glass on the end table. His fingers began to use it to wet Francesca's parched lips. He raised her jersey and put another ice cube on her warm supple body as he watched it melt slowly down towards her stomach. Francesca awoke to his sumptuous actions. She felt the passions of his desire as he embraced her. Within moments she experienced another perfect rapture from one of Damien's skillful maneuvers. She knew that this couldn't last forever, and reality set in as Monday morning arrived.

Damien explained a shorter route home. She kissed him goodbye.

Traffic was at a standstill during Monday morning rush hour. After a long drive she finally progressed to her exit and soon drove to the back alley to the side of her place. She raced to change her clothes and replenished the supplies for Dizzy.

As Monday night came, Francesca was driving past Piedmont Park towards the lights of The View Restaurant at "The Meadow" on 10th St on her way to visit Julie and Ron. Soon she passed the intersection of Virginia-Highland then turned right onto Lanier. Unfortunately, there were already two cars in the narrow driveway. Francesca had to go down the street around the grassy median and found a parking space.

The Peters rented the first floor of the 1940's style house with a simple front porch. She loved the giant tree that would hang over the front yard to give it shade on hot days. Francesca hadn't spoken to them since last week. She was greeted with hugs at the entrance of their house. The conversation started with an update of Angie's condition and the trip with Brian. Julie and Ron then questioned Francesca about her disappearance during the weekend. She informed them that she had been with Damien, the guy she had met through the personal ad. Ron cautioned her on moving so quickly since she had been a "Bum Magnet" when it came to men in her past. Julie was more tactful and was glad she was finally happy but wanted them to meet Damien. Francesca stated she wanted to wait another couple of weeks before he was brought onto the masses.

It was getting late and Francesca was about to leave when the doorbell rang. Brian had missed dinner with them due to prep work for a court appearance tomorrow. They asked Francesca to stay longer but she wanted to get to sleep at a decent hour and declined. Brian followed her out to her car, and she updated him on the Damien situation. Brian's advice was the same as Julie and Ron about meeting Damien.

Francesca promised to set up an evening with everyone. Brian gave her a hug and kiss on the cheek before he crossed the street. Luckily, it was less than ten minutes to get to her place.

She was about to go to bed when the phone rang. Angie inquired about the status of the new adventure with Damien. Francesca had spoken with her during the weekend from his place to make sure she didn't have to make another trip out of town. Angie said she was feeling better and her recovery was going well. Francesca promised to call her in the next few days to check on her. She barely kept her eyes opened and went to bed after the conversation with Angie. Damien had called early before she went to work the next morning. He invited Francesca to dinner for that night at seven thirty. Since he had been working late the last week, he told her to wait for his call before she headed for his place.

After work Francesca had completed her preparations to spend the night at Damien's place. She watched television and waited for his call. It was eight, Francesca assumed Damien worked late. She called his job and was informed he had left at seven fifteen. She decided to wait awhile longer before calling his place. She was thinking since he was making dinner, he could have stopped by the store to pick up a few things. Francesca realized it was eight-thirty as a new program came on the television. She called his place and left a message on the machine. Her clock chimed nine and still no word from Damien.

Francesca was mad since he lived fifteen minutes from work and the store was around the corner from his townhouse. At nine thirty she left another message on his machine. By ten Francesca was worried, maybe Damien had been in an accident, was hurt, sick, or did he stand her up! She thought things were good between them. Finally, at eleven-thirty the phone rang, and she answered it.

"Hello!"

"Hello Francesca, this is Damien."

"Yes," she responded coldly.

"I'm sorry I didn't call you sooner," Damien responded.

"Where have you been?"

"I got free tickets at the last minute to the Braves' against St. Louis Cardinals' game from my boss. I went straight to the game from work. I was going to call you from the stadium and ask you to meet me since you told me you are a Cards' fan. Suddenly, I realized I didn't have your number with me."

"Oh really!" Francesca abruptly responded.

"The game was amazing with outfielder Deion Sanders doing two home runs off the Cards' Watson in the third and fifth innings.

It was a close game but unfortunately, the Braves lost four to five!" Damien stated with enthusiasm.

Ah, too bad!" The sarcasm in Francesca's responses became more intense.

"I really enjoyed the game." He appeared to finally recognize her anger, "You really don't give a damn about the game or if I enjoyed it. Do you?"

"No, not really." Francesca was trying to control her emotions.

"I'm sorry for not seeing you tonight." Damien's apology seemed genuine.
"I guess I could accept your apology. If you want, I can still come over and spend the rest of the night with you."

"Well, (Damien paused) that isn't possible."

"Do you want to come over here?" Francesca was willing to believe his explanation.

"No, I had a message from Tina. I have to straighten out a banking problem in the early morning in Charleston. I'm going to take off from work tomorrow. I'm about to leave in a few minutes for Charleston."

There was a silence from Francesca.

"Are you still there?" Damien inquired.

Francesca realized it was past midnight and he wouldn't arrive in Charleston until four-thirty or five in the morning. It was obvious whose house he would be staying at until the bank opened at nine. She took a deep breath before responding to Damien. "Not only did you stand me up, but you are adding insult to injury by running off to be with Tina at five in the morning!" Her tone was turning to sarcasm again.

"Trust me, I'll probably sleep on her sofa for a couple of hours then after our banking I'll head back to Atlanta." Damien's smooth voice captivated her to calmness.

"Will I see you when you get back?" Francesca couldn't help herself and tried to display a blind faith in him.

"Yes, I'll be back early. I have to go. Goodbye Francesca," Damien quickly ended the conversation.

Francesca was drained after the emotional roller coaster with Damien. Instead of remembering April 19th as just another Tuesday, it would be the day she lost a little trust in Damien. Perhaps she shouldn't have accused him of running back to the arms of his former lover, but she was hurt and angry. Francesca would be more cautious of her statements in the future and attempt not to appear as possessive towards him. Maybe the break was good for them since they had been practically joined at the hip during the last weekend. Francesca was still upset but after an hour was able to sleep.

Brian called Francesca at work the next day and invited her to dinner since he had missed their last engagement at the Peters' house. She thought about Damien's promise to be back early from his trip but wasn't going to put herself through another night of waiting by the phone for him. She accepted Brian's invitation and met him after work. The two had a great time of relaxation during dinner. They made plans to go to the movies Saturday. They decided to invite Julie and Ron to go with them.

It had been a hot day and Francesca was glad she had been in the air condition theatre. She turned up the speed on her ceiling fan to cool down her living room when she arrived home. Just as she stretched out on her sofa the phone rang. It was the first time she had heard from Damien since their conversation late Tuesday night. He was apologetic that he hadn't contacted her sooner. Apparently, he had been exhausted from his late-night drive and since his banking business took longer than anticipated he decided to spend the night in Charleston. Damien arrived back but had worked late the rest of the week. Damien proclaimed he missed Francesca and wanted her to spend the rest of the weekend with him. She declined stating she had to work the day shift on Sunday at the hospital. Francesca could have joined him after her shift but felt she shouldn't appear desperate or needy as she had during their last conversation. Damien ended the conversation with wishing her a nice weekend and that he would call her during the week.

Several days had passed since the weekend and Francesca had recently left her office to meet with a client. Unfortunately, when she arrived the client had just called his receptionist and left Francesca a message with his apologies requesting to reschedule with her. She called her boss to update him on the situation but due to the lateness of the afternoon and upcoming rush hour traffic he suggested she make it an early day. Francesca took her boss' advice and went home.

The phone rang as she entered her place. She ran to catch it before the machine would pick it up. Damien's tone seemed surprised to hear her voice. He said he was expecting to leave a message to take her to an early dinner since he was in her area. Francesca then explained the details of her early arrival home. Damien offered to pick her up. Not wanting to seem too desperate she paused a moment before accepting his invitation. Francesca freshened up by brushing her teeth and touching up her make-up. Within minutes the doorbell rang before she could change her clothes. She opened the door and Damien was standing on the porch holding a dozen yellow roses and a bottle of red wine. Her initial reaction was to embrace him, but she controlled her actions. She invited him into her place and closed the door as he went towards the sofa. He put the bottle down on the coffee table and presented her with the bouquet of roses.

"I cannot apologize enough for the events of the past few days. I hope you accept the flowers and my promise it won't happen again. I wouldn't blame you if you said no but can we continue to see each other?" Damien displayed his faint smile.

"How can I say no after such a sincere gesture? Thank you for the roses and wine. But in the future, promise you'll have my number on you and anymore out of town visits won't be in the middle of the night to be with Tina." Francesca insisted.

"I promise!"

Francesca took the roses from his hand and put them on the table next to the wine. Before she had a chance to get a vase, Damien gently took her hand and turned her around to face him. He embraced her tenderly as she reciprocated his actions with a deep long kiss. They were soon involved in another sensually satisfying lovemaking session which ended in Francesca's bedroom. The alarm awoke them at six the next morning and Damien quickly dressed. He gave Francesca a passionate kiss, promised to return tonight, and flew out of her place. She hoped he wouldn't be late for work since he had to stop by The Pointe first to take a shower and change his clothes. Francesca took a shower and turned on the stereo to jazz music as she finished getting ready for work. Once again, she went to her job on little sleep, but she didn't care since Damien had redeemed himself with her.

Francesca was looking forward to her next rendezvous with Damien which they had planned for that evening. When she returned to the office after lunch, the receptionist had a message for her from Damien. Francesca called him at work, and he informed her he would have to work late and didn't want her to wait up for him. She was disappointed but appreciated his effort in notifying her promptly of the situation. He promised to make it up to her over the weekend. Francesca felt this could be a long-lasting relationship since he was being more considerate of her feelings.

CHAPTER NINE

Damien's assistance at her place had helped Francesca to a speedy recuperation in less than four weeks. The swelling had gone from her nose and cheek. But there was still a soreness to her face when pressure was applied. On the upside she had lost twenty pounds over the past few weeks due to her special diet. She had become more mobile since she downgraded from crutches to the cane and a boot for her ankle injury. The doctor told her she was recovering at a great pace. However, as Francesca looked at herself in the mirror, she felt any beauty she had in the past that had attracted Damien to her was gone.

Francesca was looking forward to returning to work and her hospitals shifts even though she still would have to use a cane to maneuver herself. If she needed further help Brian would assist her. Brian had originally planned on being out of town for only a week. But his client needed him to make numerous trips over the past weeks. Damien could return to his life without her as he had requested before she was injured. Francesca was feeling a case of cabin fever which Damien had sensed. He had invited her to the movies, and she was expecting him soon. She wasn't going to look into this outing as anything special. She had to remind herself sometimes a movie is just a movie.

The doorbell rang. Damien greeted her with a kiss on her uninjured cheek. He assisted her down the walkway to his car. Francesca laughed at the sarcastic comments Damien made about the movie. She felt great since she hadn't been able to relax in weeks. Damien escorted Francesca back into her place and asked for a cup of coffee. She was surprised that he wanted to stay but thought maybe he wanted the coffee to be able to stay awake for his drive home. He went to the kitchen and returned to the living room with two cups for them. She thanked him and he sat close to her on the sofa.

Damien put down his cup and began to hold her hand, "I'm sorry for all you have been through these past weeks. My statement to you before the incident had been harsh and I should have been more tactful towards your feelings. I wanted you to understand that considering my circumstances I thought it would be best for us to make a clean break. If I had let Brian know the truth you probably wouldn't have been hurt."

"I really appreciated all you have done for me during my recovery. I realize it interrupted your routine. I don't blame you for my injuries, there is no way for you to predict it would turn out that way."

"I miss being with you Francesca," Damien was staring into her eyes.

"What do you mean? You have seen me almost every day since I have been home from the hospital," Francesca expressed confusion.

"I miss being close with you. Is it too soon but I want to be intimate with you again?" Damien's compassionate tone was starting to affect her judgement.

"I'm at a loss. I thought you never wanted to touch me again and the time we spent together recently was due to sympathy," Francesca was attempting to stay in control of her emotions.

"I still do care, but it is entirely up to you," Damien responded in his sultry voice that made Francesca let her defenses down.

It had been a while since they had been together, but Francesca was still attracted to him. She answered his request with an embrace and a loving kiss. Damien picked her up and gallantly took her to the bedroom for an amorous night of passion.

During the night Damien had shown gentleness with her injuries. He gave her a goodbye kiss as the sun was rising. Francesca wasn't sure if the night meant a change of heart in his plans or it was a continuation of the lust they had shared since they had met. She took a shower carefully with her injured leg. The phone rang as she was dressing. Damien wanted to see her for dinner, and he offered to cook at her place. She agreed and continued to prepare for her first day back at work.

She was grateful to get back in the hustle of the business world, but she was extremely tired by the time she got home. Damien was waiting for her on the front porch with groceries in his arms. He prepared a wonderful meal for them. He then saw the tension in her face from the day. Damien gave her a soothing body massage which made her reach screams of ecstasy. He chose not to stay the night stating he wanted her to be able to get plenty of rest for work the next day. Damien made plans with her to attend a charity benefit for Saturday night.

Francesca drove into the gates of The Pointe and was excited about attending the benefit with Damien. He greeted her outside and then escorted her to his car. They arrived at the event and she enjoyed the evening of listening to the jazz concert. When they returned to his place, she wasn't sure if he would invite her in, but he did. He started a long conversation with her about the possibilities of any future encounters with each other. She wanted to be with him and was willing to give it another chance. He asked her to spend the night and she agreed even though she had to do a partial hospital shift in the late morning. In the morning Francesca was greeted by Damien's gentle caresses of her body but soon had to leave to go home and prepare for her shift. He said he would call her later in the day. They kissed as she left his place.

Francesca was waiting for Damien's call before she went to bed. The call finally came.

"Francesca, I really enjoyed being close to you again. I've been thinking about this all day and I feel maybe we shouldn't have started being intimate again. You know my circumstances. I think we just need space."

"You mean you need space!" Francesca's defiance was apparent.

"I have to go. Goodbye Francesca."

"Goodbye Damien." Francesca was bewildered by Damien's statements. She was conflicted between anger or sorrow!

CHAPTER
TEN

Francesca had plans with Damien for him to meet Brian, Julie, and Ron during the May Festival in the Park weekend. Francesca loved this festival since she had met Brian at one of these events several years ago. Her friends were all going to stay at her place. It would be a tight fit but between the sofa and sleeping bags they would make it work. She was slightly nervous about the interrogation Damien would have to endure from her friends. However, she was excited for them to share time with her new companion.

Friday night came quickly, and everyone was at her place except Damien. She assumed he must have been caught in traffic since he was driving in from the suburbs. The phone rang, it was Damien explaining he had to go out of town for the weekend to be with a sick family member. Francesca was disappointed but didn't want to be possessive by asking him too many questions. He ended the conversation by saying he would call her in a few days. She hung up the phone and gave Damien's apologies to everyone for canceling out.

She decided she would go with the flow instead of getting ballistic over the situation. The next few days she enjoyed the various concerts, spending time with her friends, and meeting new people. By the end of the weekend, she met a new friend by the name of Keisha White. Keisha was a slender twenty-four-year-old black woman who was a computer programmer. She seemed to get along with Francesca's circle of friends especially Julie and Ron since they were in the same career.

Maybe it was the lack of sleep or too much of a good time but by Tuesday morning Francesca felt burned out. She needed a mental health day from her job. Damien had called her at home after being unable to reach her at work. She updated him on her great weekend and new friend, Keisha. He said his family member was doing better and apologized again for his sudden departure out of town. Damien wanted to see her after work, but she declined. They instead made plans to meet at his place the next evening.

On Wednesday night Damien was still dressed in his business attire upon her arrival. The table wasn't set nor was there an aroma of food that usually greeted her senses. Damien instead took her out to a romantic bistro in the elegant Vining's section of the city. He took the Paces Ferry exit off the Perimeter loop. She was excited after the eight-minute drive to arrive at Gregory's Restaurant. The violin serenade, candles, and dimmed lights seemed to put Damien in an amorous mood as he held her hand from across the table.

They had a wonderful discussion including future plans for him to finally meet her friends. Francesca repaid him for his thoughtfulness by a night of unselfish devotion she hoped would satisfy his innermost needs.

Brian called Francesca the next day and asked if she would join the group for Italian at The Underground. She was to meet them at seven but decided to be spontaneous and invited Damien. He accepted but she decided to be on the cautious side and not tell her friends in case he should cancel again. Francesca rushed up 10th Street past Peachtree Street to the Midtown MARTA Station. She quickly went down the stairs towards the Red Line Southbound train as it was pulling up. Upon entering the train, she saw there were no seats available. Luckily, she would only have to stand holding the pole for four stops. She exited at the Five Points Station she tried to enter the tunnel into The Underground section but was detoured outside to cross at Alabama Street. She ran down the stairs to the main entrance of The Underground. She entered through the glass doors.

To her astonishment Damien was waiting in the historical brick archway of the restaurant. They entered the lobby with their hands interlocked. Three of her four friends had grins on their faces. She hadn't expected Kenny but figured one day he would meet Damien. Francesca made the introductions. They sat at their table and Damien was questioned by the group. Damien seemed to roll with the punches and showed his charming qualities to her friends. At the end of the dinner Julie pulled Francesca aside and gave her approval of the new relationship.

After dinner Damien gave Francesca a ride home so she wouldn't have to deal with the subway at night. She was about to get out of his car when he gave her a goodnight kiss. She thought he was coming in, but it was obvious he had other plans in mind. She said goodnight and quickly ran inside her place.

Francesca was slightly annoyed by Damien's parting actions last night. Maybe she was being too needy with his time since he did finally meet and charm her friends. Perhaps she needed a change of scenery. She recalled Angie was doing better and would probably be up for visitors. Francesca packed her bag after a conversation with Angie on the phone. The mountains were pleasant this time of the year and Francesca was enjoying her stress-free weekend. She updated Angie with the past events of her relationship with Damien. As they were looking through gift shops, Angie showed a mountainous postcard to Francesca and suggested she send it to Damien with the message: "The weather is nice, wish you were here!" Although it was tempting, Francesca declined. Damien wasn't a bad guy. He gave her flowers, he either cooked or paid for meals at elegant restaurants, and always apologized.

After a peaceful weekend, it was hard to adjust to the work week. Francesca decided to call Damien since she hadn't heard from him in several days. He had been busy working on a major project for his job and hadn't had any spare time. Francesca suggested they see each other over the weekend. He said he would have to get back with her. She was becoming more dependent of his attention and was wondering if he was feeling the pressure of it.

Friday afternoon Francesca called Damien to get an update of possible plans. He had met his deadline and explained he could spend part of the weekend with her but had special plans for

Sunday. That evening she was glad to be in the comforts of his place again and enjoyed a leisurely evening with him. Damien received a phone call from his brother confirming plans to spend Mother's Day with their father. Francesca understood why his plans couldn't be changed. She told him she admired his compassionate actions he had towards his father in honoring the memory of his mother. Damien looked deep into her eyes as he thanked her for the compliment and cuddled with her on the sofa.

It was early Saturday morning as Damien awoke on the sofa still holding Francesca in his arms. He gently tried to get up and stretch without waking Francesca but was unable. She followed him to his bedroom where she promptly fell onto his bed and went back to sleep. Damien took a shower, dressed, and attempted to wake Francesca. She eventually left the bed and showered before their day of outings. Damien promised her brunch but first had to make his weekly trip to the dry cleaners. It reminded her of his impeccable taste in clothing and he was starting to include her in on his regular routine. They ended the day with dinner at a sidewalk café by the park.

Upon their return to The Pointe, Damien suggested they retire to bed since they both had early commitments in the morning. Francesca thought the weekend had been romantic with hand holding, long walks, and cuddling even though they hadn't been physically intimate. Damien set the alarm and slid into bed with Francesca. He rolled over to give her a brief hug and goodnight kiss. He whispered about the aroma of her perfume he appeared to inhale as he sucked her neck. A night of passion evoked between them. The alarm went off at six and Francesca jumped into the shower first to prepare for her hospital shift. They were both out the door by six-thirty with Damien headed towards his father's place and Francesca to the city.

At the end of her shift, Francesca was paged to the front desk. When she arrived, Brian and Kenny pleasantly surprised her. They wanted to treat her to an early dinner. Even though she had been attracted at one time to Kenny's muscular body standing at six-two, that was in the past, and now she had Damien in her life. Brian had sponsored Kenny for his membership into Omega Psi Phi since there was no longer active rushing. They were proud to be part of The Divine Nine at the only all male HBCU (Historical Black College/University) of Morehouse College.

Both men were well versed and willing to share the history of it. They had shared with her it was the first international fraternity organization to be founded on the campus of a HBCU at Howard University in 1930. It was apparent they lived by the Omega motto, "Friendship is essential to the Soul." Kenny and Brian had remained friends since their college days. Brian's Big Brother duties didn't end with his Morehouse days. She decided it would be good to have a change, and she always had amusing outings with these two in the past.

After her evening out, Francesca arrived home and was going to check on Damien to make sure he had a safe trip. But she remembered he stated he wouldn't be home until late. She then decided to get a good night's sleep since she would be going to Damien's place after work tomorrow.

Monday night Francesca had dinner with Damien and watched a video. Throughout the evening it seemed like Damien was preoccupied. She wanted to inquire but thought maybe visiting his father had brought up painful memories of his mother's death. The silence was finally broken with Damien's announcement that he would be going on vacation starting Friday and be gone for a week. Francesca had a surprised look on her face. To soften the blow, Damien was asking her out for dinner Thursday night to try to make-up for his impending absence. She accepted but wanted to ask numerous questions. Francesca decided to wait until Thursday once she had thought of a non-judgmental manner to address the issue. She was quiet as they went to his bedroom to sleep.

They arrived at Francesca's place Thursday night after dining out. Damien seemed in a solemn mood and it concerned her. She sat on the sofa, but Damien remained standing. Before Francesca could inquire about his vacation, Damien began to speak without much emotion.

"Francesca, I'm spending my vacation taking Tina's boys camping for the week. This was planned before I met you. They had become attached to me when we lived together. I also feel this would be a good time for us to split up since it has been getting too serious between us. I feel you want more than I can give to you at this time."

There was a brief silence as she tried to compose her words into a coherent statement.

"Damien be honest with me, are you still in love with Tina or is this your way of having a clear conscious so you can sleep with her again when you stay in Charleston?" Francesca tried to take control of the conversation.

85

"We have a history for years. I still care about the well-being of her family and feel I can't totally abandon them. There is something I want to tell you that I haven't shared with anybody-else. In the beginning of my relationship with Tina, I was supposed to pick her up from work but was running late due to being with a former girlfriend. It was pouring down rain and Tina crossed King Street to flag down a taxi at The Omni Hotel but was struck by a car. She received numerous injuries including a permanent limp in her leg and she has to use a cane to walk. I feel responsible and must make sure that her family always is safe."

"I had no idea. I'm sorry for her condition but unless she is moving to Atlanta, I feel we could work it out." Francesca was standing her ground.

"I just need time to figure things out. I still think a split at this time is best for everyone. I need to go."

Damien headed towards the door and looked back at her to say goodbye. Francesca had put her face in her hands to hide her crying. She hadn't realized until that moment, but she had fallen in love with him. Damien walked back then sat on the sofa next to her. He put his arm around her while rubbing her back. She looked up at him and wanted to say something but was speechless. Damien brushed the tears from her cheeks. He slowly kissed her on the cheek then tenderly on the lips. Francesca wanted to reject his advances but needed to feel the comfort of his touches one last time. He guided her into the bedroom where they shared a night of gentle lovemaking. Damien parted in the morning without a word but instead gave her an embrace before he exited through the front door.

Francesca couldn't let her personal life affect her performance at work. At least she would be busy this weekend with her firm's new client. They were a corporate sponsor of a new festival called "Music Midtown." Francesca would have to be on site both Friday and Saturday. She was amazed at the range of performers. Her company was in charge of coordinating the concerts on various stages during the event. Francesca attempted to hide her enthusiasm as she could have literally touched these artists she had grown to love through the years. Her breath was taken away when Joan Baez and later James Brown did their sets. She briefly thought that Damien would have loved the concerts. During the event, she ran into Keisha and they went out clubbing after the festival on Saturday night. As the week progressed, Francesca spoke with Brian and Julie but didn't inform them of the break-up with Damien. They had given approval of him and she was hoping after his vacation, Damien might change his mind.

It had been over a week since he left her, and she couldn't help but wonder if he had made it home safely. Francesca could no longer suppress her urge and called him. She wasn't sure what his reaction would be but maybe they could be friends like the relationship she has with Kenny. Damien was receptive to hearing from her and invited her to his place. When she entered his townhouse, he closed the door, and they were immediately enthralled in sensual movements which led them to his bedroom. Afterwards, he said it wouldn't work for them to be just friends since he had missed her. Francesca was relieved by Damien's change of heart. She didn't want to scare him away by her feelings of love until she was sure of the stability of their relationship.

It had been several days since her last encounter with Damien. Friday night Francesca walked to their favorite restaurant at the park to meet him for dinner. He had brought her a yellow rose. The View Restaurant sat at the corner of 10th Street and Monroe. They entered the main inside dining area. Damien requested outside seating. This place had justly earned its name with the gorgeous evening scenery of the Midtown skyline highlighted by the lamp posts lighting the path of "The Meadow." It was a perfect meal complete with a flaming baked Alaska.

They exited up the steep staircase to the parking lot. She loved the architectural designs of the building especially the tower at the top enhanced by the golden glow of the lighting. They had walked to his car and he gave her the keys to drive. Damien said he was too tired to drive and hadn't brought a change of clothing otherwise he would stay at her place. Francesca was surprised and nervous as she drove his elegant car but felt a slight thrill. She stopped by her place to pack her overnight bag then fed Dizzy. She kept glancing at Damien as she exited for the Perimeter, but his eyes were closed. Upon entering The Pointe, the guard was on break and she gently nudged Damien to code them into the gate. Instead of getting out of the car to go to the keypad, he gave her the code. As the gates opened, she realized he was giving her more access to his life.

The next evening still at his place Francesca was feeling confident about the status of her relationship and decided to be spontaneous with Damien. She went to his closet. Francesca handed him a change of clothes. She told him he had fifteen minutes to get ready. Damien gave Francesca a bewildered look but complied with her wishes. She asked for the keys to his car which he handed to her. They left with Damien asking numerous questions about their destination, but Francesca only replied he should be more patient. She exited at International Boulevard and turned into the parking garage.

Damien appeared not to have a clue of the final destination until they walked around the corner and he saw The Hard Rock Café. A smile came across his face as he gave her a kiss on the cheek. Francesca explained she was given a bonus for her work on the festival and the evening was her treat. He had always paid anytime they went out. Damien had mentioned in the past that he liked the atmosphere of the restaurant. The walls were lined with memorabilia from the music greats. Damien's love of various artists was expressed as he made comments about their autographed items. He especially loved the Ella Fitzgerald, B.B. King, and Tina Turner displays. The place was packed but the wait seemed to go quickly while they listened to the "Old School" and rock music in the background.

As the server approached their table, Francesca saw a familiar face. An energetic mocha complexion, well-built, twenty-five- year-old male who stood shy of six-feet gave her a hug.

Damien's eyes widened until Francesca did the introductions. Lionel Blake worked part-time at the restaurant and had decided to return to school for his MBA. They had met during one of the festivals at Piedmont Park. Damien's raised eyebrows showed his uncomfortable mood with the closeness she had with Lionel. But after some humorous anecdotes from their server, Damien realized he didn't need to be concerned. Before Francesca left, she promised Lionel they would get together soon.

Damien showed his appreciation of Francesca's surprise when they returned to his place. The next morning Damien discussed plans for the next weekend since it was Francesca's birthday. She had said for him not to make a fuss but secretly hoped he would make it memorable.

CHAPTER ELEVEN

Francesca knew Damien's pending situation but still felt if he would consider her alternative plan, they could have a future together. She wasn't going to beg however, she had to decide how much compromising she would be. Francesca had finished prep for Angie's visit. After their brief separation, plans were made with Damien for Saturday night, but she wasn't excepting him to show up. The doorbell rang and Angie had arrived from the upstate. As she was about to escort Angie inside, Brian pulled up in his black BMW. He exited his car and briskly ran up the steps. He gave Angie a hug. They had decided to go out on Friday and invited Francesca to accompany them.

The group entered the house then dropped the luggage and enjoyed a drink. The phone rang as the three were about to leave for dinner. Francesca went to her bedroom for privacy as she heard Damien's voice on the cordless phone. He inquired if Angie had arrived and if he would still be welcomed for their outing tomorrow night. Francesca was no longer surprised by anything he did. She stated since she didn't want to play twenty questions with Angie, she would appreciate it if he would keep his promise. She told him the time and place to meet them which he agreed to be there on time. Francesca returned from the bedroom and attempted to be casual about her phone conversation with Damien. It was apparent to her friends that she was preoccupied but they were respectful of her privacy. They left for an evening of dinner and sightseeing on Peachtree Street. At the end of the evening Brian said his goodbyes and confirmed their date for tomorrow night.

Brian had driven Francesca and Angie to the restaurant where Damien was waiting for them in the lobby. He introduced himself to Angie, who had only spoken to him on the phone during Francesca's recovery. Ficarello's was a casual restaurant famous for numerous pasta entrees in the Vining's section. The tables were covered with red cloth and a simple floral arrangement served as a centerpiece. There were photos of Italy hung on the red brick walls. Damien was his typical charming self, but Angie appeared to be weary of his actions. As they were parting the restaurant, Damien asked for a moment of Francesca's time. He wanted them to go somewhere to talk privately and he would bring her home later. Francesca was hesitant but thought it would be nice to give Angie and Brian some time alone at her place. Since they were a few miles from The Pointe, Damien suggested they go to his place.

Francesca turned her head, she looked sideways at the scenery of traffic and buildings as they entered the Perimeter from Paces Ferry. She felt her stomach tighten as they exited to S. Cobb Drive. The silence of the car ride had been deafening. She felt her emotions must remain calm. They arrived at the townhouse and Francesca decided to let Damien plead his case. He said he enjoyed being with her but couldn't make a lifetime commitment. Francesca knew it was wrong to give in but her desires to have him in her life kept overcoming her common sense. She melted as he touched her hand and stroked her cheek before they tenderly kissed on the lips. He stirred such intense emotions in her soul she couldn't resist him.

The next morning Francesca and Damien awoke embracing each other. She informed him she had to get home due to her plans with Angie. Damien quickly dressed and drove her to Midtown. He gave her a kiss and made plans to see her after Angie left Atlanta. Francesca couldn't help but feel guilty about spending the night with Damien. She wondered if her actions needed to be justified to Angie. Before she opened the door, she took a deep breath imagining Angie would be waiting like a parent when a teenager had missed curfew.

Angie was still asleep as Francesca took a shower. She stretched out on the sofa and went back to sleep for a couple of hours but was awoke by Angie's brewed coffee. Angie questioned Francesca on her evening with Damien and warned her she didn't trust him. She said enjoy it while you can but guys like that aren't long range planners. Francesca thanked her for her concern and dropped the subject. She heard the doorbell and answered it. Brian and Kenny had brought groceries to make brunch. They had a nice, relaxed time but it was getting late. Angie had to get back to pick-up her kids from her ex-husband. Before everyone left Francesca's place, Kenny informed her if ever she needed someone to talk to, he would be there for her. Francesca knew he was attempting to protect her from any pain. She thanked him for his offer with a kiss on the cheek. Then she tried to reassure him her life was fine.

The next evening Damien came over to her place for pizza and a movie. It was a quiet time for them considering the past ones together. It was getting late when he announced he had an early morning for work. They kissed and he left without incident. She was thankful to have peace between them again.

CHAPTER TWELVE

Damien had promised Francesca that he would devote the whole weekend to her birthday. She raced out of work Friday and went straight to The Pointe. Damien was preparing dinner for them and had romantic soul music playing on the stereo to set the mood. After the meal, Damien attempted to find a program for them on the television. He finally came across a bad horror flick with a girl in tight jeans. She dropped her keys and a psycho killer chased her.

Francesca was amused by the movie and made a sarcastic comment, "Why didn't she put the keys in her pocket?"

"How the hell could they fit in there, her jeans are painted on!" Damien playfully responded.

"Oh, you like her backside?"

"Oh well, I hadn't noticed but some guys like that sort of girl, but not me!" he said in a semi-serious tone.

97

"Good save!" Francesca exclaimed.

The movie wasn't over, but Damien noticed it was midnight and told Francesca to close her eyes. He left the sofa as she cooperated with his request. Damien returned and suddenly she felt a coldness melting down her exposed neckline as he was kissing her with the taste of ice cream across her lips. He proceeded to open her blouse and continue the flow of motion. Francesca hadn't experienced these sensations and was surprised at Damien's adventurous nature. The next morning, she couldn't imagine what he would be doing to top last night's session.

Saturday night Damien took Francesca to Segreto Notte for her birthday dinner. Before the coffee came, Damien gave an elegantly wrapped package to her. She tried to curb her enthusiasm as she ripped it open. To her astonishment Damien had given her several gifts. She saw a heart shaped porcelain musical jewelry case decorated with a painted yellow rose on top. It was filled with gold heart earrings and matching gold charm bracelet. Francesca was elated, she jumped up to give Damien a kiss.

They finished their evening at the restaurant and returned to The Pointe, which was a short drive. Damien told her to sit on the sofa as he went upstairs to the bedroom. He returned with a bouquet of yellow roses and serenaded her with his saxophone. Francesca was impressed with his musical ability when he performed a song from her favorite R&B singer. She thought nothing could spoil her birthday. After he had finished his harmonious number, they decided to adjourn to his bedroom. Damien decided to put his sax in the case downstairs first. Francesca was lying in the bed awaiting his arrival when she heard the phone ring. He answered it downstairs and as she heard part of the conversation, she knew it was Tina. Damien was only on the phone a few minutes then joined Francesca. She wasn't amused by the interruption. Damien noticed she had turned her back on him.

"Oh, so you are going to ignore me. It was only a phone call. I'm sorry it happened on your birthday. I can't help who calls me!" Damien pleaded.

There was no response from Francesca.

"At least you are giving me something, even if it is only your back!" He responded sarcastically.

Damien gently gave her one of his infamous massages in an attempt to turn her towards him. Francesca gave into his manipulative maneuvers. His strong hands creeped between her

99

thighs but stopped for a moment. Her breaths increased which seemed to motivate Damien. He continued further with stroked motions into her zone. She felt the moistness increased when his fingers hit the ultimate spot. Her body shook. Damien eased into Francesca's inner being. Each of his movements culminated in her screams with each climax. Afterwards they were resting, she noticed he had a faint smile as he sighed.

She inquired about his sounds, "What are you thinking about?"

"I'm still basking in the effervescent afterglow!" Damien responded in his seductive voice.

They both laughed and continued in their embrace until morning. Damien had kept his promise and given her a birthday she would never forget. Francesca didn't want this serenity to end but they had to return to the real world of their careers.

She had made plans to take Brian out for his birthday during the week at his favorite restaurant at The Underground. Brian couldn't help but notice the tranquil mood she was displaying. Francesca informed him about the dinner, roses, serenade, and gifts

Damien had bestowed on her. Brian conveyed his blessing towards her relationship but still cautioned her falling too hard for Damien. Francesca was optimistic about the future. During dinner Francesca started to feel queasy. Brian drove her home since she had taken the subway. He was concerned and asked if she had been sick or tired other times? She replied that ever since she took the sick day last month, she hadn't had much energy. Francesca assumed it was due to lack of sleep because of Damien. Brian informed her that it was obvious what was causing the problem if she would admit it. He made her promise to make a doctor's appointment as soon as possible to confirm his suspicions. She agreed and gave him a hug as he left. Francesca wasn't going to panic until after her confirmation of the problem from a doctor.

The next evening Francesca sat on her sofa as she tried to process the doctor's diagnosis. She thought the proper precautions had been taken. Francesca had to make the call to Damien but wasn't sure of his reaction. She finally dialed his number and waited nervously for him to answer.

"Hello."

"Damien, I need to see you tonight."

"Unfortunately, I have to finish a report for work. Tomorrow would be better for me."

"I wouldn't insist but it's really important we see each other. I went to the doctor today," Francesca's tone was persistent.

"Are you hurt or ill? Is there anything I can do for you?" Damien responded in a concerned tone.

"I'm pregnant," Francesca proclaimed.

"I'm sure we can work out a solution we can both live with. I'll have to get back to you. Goodbye Francesca," Damien's voice had changed from concerned to a business tone.

Before she had a chance to respond he had hung up. Francesca had to assume that she may be doing this on her own. Damien had said he felt the relationship was getting too serious in the past. She had always wanted to be a mother but after several miscarriages during her marriage to Tom, she thought this issue wouldn't enter her life again. Her emotions were raw thinking this was her last shot. Francesca listened to some Oleta Adams music for the next hour when she heard the doorbell.

She jumped up from the sofa hoped it might be Damien. Instead, she opened the door to Brian. He admitted since he hadn't heard any news, he assumed he was correct, and she would probably need a friend. Francesca informed him she had already contacted Damien about the baby. She wasn't completely truthful with Brian about Damien's reaction and only stated they were taking time to weigh their options. Brian emphasized that she shouldn't let anyone force her into a decision she would regret later in life. Francesca was grateful for his brotherly advice but requested he not share the news with their other friends. Brian agreed and offered to stay longer if she needed to talk. She thanked him for his thoughtfulness but was extremely tired and wanted to go to bed. Brian gave her a hug and said he would check on her during the week. Francesca had a restless sleep during the night. She was tempted to call in sick but decided work would be a good distraction for her.

Saturday morning Francesca had accepted an offer from Keisha to go shopping since she hadn't heard from Damien. As Keisha was driving on the Perimeter, another car forced their car towards a construction barrier near the Cobb Parkway exit. Keisha tried to stop the car from crashing into the orange barriers but instead hit them with full force. There was water exploding over the road. Keisha's car finally stopped off the embankment after hydroplaning. They were both conscious however, Francesca began feeling sharp pains in her abdominal area. She tried to remain calm while she awaited help but wondered if the baby was alright.

The doctor completed the examination of Francesca and informed her they would have to perform a Dilation and Curettage (D&C), since her pregnancy was no longer viable. When the nurse asked for an emergency contact Francesca couldn't think. She felt as though she was in a bad dream and wished someone would wake her up. Even though she had only recently found out about the baby, she had decided to continue the pregnancy with or without Damien. A cruel twist of fate had made the decision for her. Francesca was finally able to give Brian's name and phone number to the nurse. After the procedure Brian was standing next to her bedside. He asked if he should contact Damien and she agreed he had a right to the details about the accident. She hoped Damien would come to be by her side immediately, but Brian was unable to reach him. Francesca asked about Keisha's condition and was told she only had minor injuries allowing her to be released. The nurse stated Keisha had stopped by the room but didn't want to disturb Francesca since she was sleeping.

Francesca was released from the hospital the next day. However, Brian still hadn't been able to locate Damien. Francesca thought he must have gone to visit his father upstate. Brian stayed at her place until finally Damien was reached. He arrived within thirty minutes of the news. Maybe she was wrong about his initial reaction to their baby. Perhaps she wouldn't have had to do it alone and his past statement was only shock. Brian said his goodbyes to them and left.

Damien sat beside Francesca on the sofa. She immediately cried while he embraced her as she was grieving the one role she would never experience... motherhood. He seemed to be compassionate to her pain then continued holding her the rest of the night.

Francesca was able to return to work after a couple of days. The Fourth of July holiday was in the near future. Damien had said a change of scenery might be nice for them. At his suggestion, she had made reservations for a chalet in the quaint mountain village of Helen. Francesca was looking forward to her first trip away with Damien. Since she lost the baby, she hadn't been sure if he was there due to pity. Francesca kept busy with her job and hospital shifts during the next few weeks.

The night before their trip she was completing last minute packing when Damien phoned. He said he was having second thoughts about the trip and maybe they should postpone it. He didn't want her to have false hopes about the significance of this time together. Francesca had to control the eruption of emotions she was experiencing. She listened quietly as he wished her a nice holiday with the parting words he would be in touch. She immediately had to cancel the chalet reservations while being charged a fee. Then she called Keisha to accept her previous invitation to a cook-out. Francesca was going to save face and not inform her friends of Damien's disappointment to her.

Francesca was having a good time at the cook-out. The Woodlands were north of Damien's place on S. Cobb Drive. Keisha's place was a lovely two-story condo subdivision surrounded by tall trees and a brook located in the rear. She was surprised to see Kenny but remembered she had introduced him to Keisha during the Park Festival. Kenny made it clear to Francesca that Keisha was only a friend to him. She was curious about the comment then wondered how many details he knew about the roller coaster relationship she had with Damien. Francesca was enjoying her conversation with Kenny so much that she accepted his offer to go out for drinks. They thanked Keisha then they left the cook-out.

Driving down the hill from Keisha's place, Francesca was waiting at the Cumberland Parkway traffic light to turn green. After it changed, within moments she went past the entrance to The Pointe and was tempted to turn but remembered that Kenny was following her car. Perhaps it was for the best that she took a break from Damien. She had been monopolizing his time since the accident. Tonight, she would spend time with an old, trusted friend.

After leaving the Midtown bar, Kenny followed her home and she invited him in for coffee. They watched a movie and fell asleep on the sofa together. The sound of a loud car starting in the parking lot awoke Francesca. She noticed it was past two in the morning and didn't have the heart to disturb Kenny. She put a blanket over him and went to sleep in her bedroom.

The aroma of coffee made Francesca jump from her bed. She grabbed her robe when she remembered Kenny had spent the night. He greeted her with a kiss on the cheek then handed her a cup of coffee. She made them breakfast as he apologized for crashing on her sofa. Francesca remembered Kenny had always been considerate of her. But she still felt a bond to be faithful to Damien. The phone rang as Kenny was freshening up in the bathroom. During her conversation with Damien, Kenny yelled for a clean towel. Damien immediately began interrogating her about who was with her. Francesca was evasive and said a friend. She wasn't in the mood for a fight and ended the conversation abruptly. She felt satisfied after she hung up the phone since the shoe was on the other foot. Damien could wonder if something was going on like the way she had felt about Tina. Kenny came out and thanked her for her hospitality. He gave her a hug and kiss then left.

Francesca cleaned up the kitchen and was about to relax on the sofa when she heard the doorbell ring. She opened the door and saw Damien with yellow roses in his hands. She couldn't believe that the sound of a man's voice in the background had made him come that quickly to her place! Francesca inquired why he was there since he had wanted space between them. Damien replied that maybe he was wrong and why shouldn't they spend time together. Francesca thanked him for the flowers, and he escorted her to the sofa. He apologized for canceling their plans but wanted to make it up to her. In her heart she felt he had a good soul. Francesca agreed to go to his place.

Upon their arrival Damien turned on music. He apologized for his actions or lack of towards the news of fatherhood. Damien gave her condolences on her loss and the trauma she had experienced from the accident. They sat on the sofa. He put his arms around her as he rocked her. His gentle nature pacified her as she remained in his cocoon until the soft jazz tape ended its first run. He gently took her face into his hands while he expressed his desire to be intimate with her. It had been weeks since she had felt his passionate touches. Her feelings for him were too strong to deny.

CHAPTER
THIRTEEN

Thursday night Francesca and Damien had finished their dinner at his place. She was reserved with her affection since he hadn't made advances their last date. Damien reminded her he wouldn't be available this weekend due to his father's October birthday party. Francesca had secretly wished she was invited but considered how volatile their relationship had been in the past, she understood. He saw the disappointment in her face and gave her a passionate kiss. She stayed in his embrace as they sat on his sofa listening to music. Francesca's eyes began to close as the urge to sleep was overcoming her. He suggested they go to bed. She stated she wanted to take a shower before going to sleep. Damien swept her up. Then he carried her up the stairs to the shower. The pulsating sensation of the waterfall beating against her back while he slowly caressed her lovingly drove Francesca to new levels of delirium.

They were cuddling in bed when they heard the phone. It was past midnight and Damien didn't answer it. He stated the machine would pick it up. The machine kept clicking. Numerous times the phone rang, stopped, and rang again. It was obvious Francesca was annoyed by the interruption.

"Why don't you answer it?" Francesca's frustrated tone was apparent.

"It's only my fax machine malfunctioning," Damien's soft tone wasn't calming her.

"It's probably Tina. She's called you late at night in the past. You might as well answer it"

Damien went to the spare bedroom next door to finally answer the phone, "I'm sorry I didn't answer the phone, Tina. I was here earlier but was in the shower. I then was in bed by ten and thought it was the fax machine. The volume on the answering machine was down since I don't like to listen to myself talk..." There was a pause while Damien listened to the other end, then he continued, "When are you coming? You can stay with my sister for my father's birthday party."

Francesca heard another pause, then a loud thump from the phone as it dropped.

"Oh damn, she is going to kill me!"

Francesca realized Damien had hung up on Tina by mistake. She couldn't help but laugh. She tried to cover her sounds with the comforter.

Damien finally reconnected with Tina, "I'm sorry, the phone slipped out of my hand." He paused to listen then continued, "Please stop shouting!"

Francesca heard him as he tried to ease the tension of the conversation by changing the subject, "My boss was impressed with my last project. — Well, I'll see you soon," Damien returned to the bedroom.

"I guess you heard that?"

"Yes, how upset was she?" Francesca tried not to show her pleasure in Tina assuming he had abruptly stopped the phone conversation.

"Oh, she was upset alright!" Damien responded laughing.

"She's coming for a visit?" Francesca asked trying to remain calm.

"My family invited her to the party," Damien attempted to explain.

"Oh, she is no longer a part of your daily life. I can't go but her and the kids are invited. They need to get over it!" Francesca turned her back on him.

"I understand you're upset but don't let something out of my control ruin our perfect evening."

Damien began to massage her back, but she didn't respond. Then he kissed her neck as his warm breath put chills up her spine. She thought maybe he was right. Tina's invitation to the party wasn't in his control. She realized her time with him was limited. Francesca turned over and succumbed to his amorous movements until sunrise.

CHAPTER FOURTEEN

A few days later Francesca noticed Damien seemed preoccupied. When she inquired if work was going well, he stated that he had to find a public relations firm to publicize a new product. Francesca immediately wanted to bid for the contract but needed to weigh if business should be mixed with pleasure. Apparently, Damien was having the same reservations since he didn't ask her directly. After a few moments, she decided to approach him. Damien paused for a few minutes. She was nervous for his response. She wondered if she had gone beyond the boundaries of their relationship.

Damien informed her that he would set-up an appointment for her to present the proposal. But it would probably be better not to disclose their dating relationship and they were strictly business acquaintances. She agreed with him and was thrilled with the possibility of being with Damien more. They spent the rest of the evening discussing his company and the new product.

The next day Francesca received the call from Damien to confirm a meeting time. She then went to her boss, Mr. Ross and explained the proposal for the new account. He was impressed with her initiative and stated he wished to be a part of the meeting.

Mr. Ross wasn't a boss to micromanage, but he saw the potential for future revenue if this one project was successful. He always showed support for his staff. The day before the big presentation came as Francesca was finalizing it with Mr. Ross. He confirmed they would meet at eight-thirty in the office and drive together. She was confident about the material but still nervous since she hadn't seen Damien's demur in the work environment. Francesca left the office and headed for The Pointe. Damien had promised her a mellow night of take-out and videos since they both had to be well rested for the meeting. Francesca entered the townhouse. Damien had everything set-up in the living room. She put her overnight bag in the bedroom, and they had a quiet evening. After the videos, they went to the bedroom as Damien set the alarm giving her extra time for the drive through Midtown rush hour traffic. Francesca went into a deep sleep. It was still dark when she felt his Panther's jersey being removed from her body and the strokes of his warm hands.

116

Neither of them said a word as he brought them both to elated bliss. They fell asleep only to hear the sound of the alarm thirty minutes later. Francesca had a hard time getting out of bed praying the shower and a cup of coffee would revive her. After she dressed, Damien escorted her to the door and kissed her goodbye.

Francesca arrived at work and immediately got another cup of coffee as she waited for Mr. Ross. Upon his arrival to the office, she grabbed her materials for the presentation. Mr. Ross offered to drive to the meeting. Francesca waited outside at the main entrance loop of Colony Square as he drove his white BMW up from the lower parking garage. They proceeded to the 14th Street NE entrance for I-75 northbound. Due to the heavy traffic, it took them almost thirty minutes to arrive to their destination on Cumberland Parkway across from the mall. They were able to find covered parking next to the building. This was Francesca's first visit to Damien's job.

They approached the large, mirrored skyscraper. She was impressed with the design and size. She was trying to hide her lack of sleep and appear alert. They entered the lobby area and went to sign in. A fifty-year-old woman was sitting behind the receptionist desk and greeted them. Mr. Ross introduced himself and before Francesca could do the same, the lady asked if she was Ms. Stefani?

117

Francesca confirmed her identity. Then the receptionist informed Francesca that Mr. Sommers had been checking for the past half hour if she had arrived. Francesca was a little embarrassed and thought so much for trying to be discreet with our employers. Damien soon appeared and introduced himself to Mr. Ross and greeted Francesca with a handshake. They followed him to the elevator. The group exited on the twelfth floor for the conference room where several other executives were present. The introductions were made, and Francesca began her presentation. She stayed calm during parts of the questioning segment which were blunt even from Damien. At the end of the meeting Francesca had showed professionalism even though she had just been intimate with Damien just a few hours before. Mr. Ross and Francesca thanked the executives for their time. In response, a promise that a decision would be made before the end of the week. Francesca and her boss returned to the office. The waiting process had begun.

The week seemed to go slow as Francesca was awaiting the call on the contract. Thursday, she received the news and informed Mr. Ross that the firm had a new client. Francesca would have to keep her feelings in control around Damien since it couldn't be anything personal during working hours. It was quitting time and she was anxious to celebrate with Damien. Francesca raced to The Pointe with her favorite bottle of wine and knocked on Damien's door. It was obvious he wasn't expecting her as she saw the suitcase in the living room. Her face turned from excitement to disappointment within seconds. Damien explained he was going to call to congratulate her however, he couldn't work on the project with her. His company was sending him to Charleston to clean-up a problem. Hopefully, he wouldn't be gone longer than a week, but he wasn't sure. Francesca sat down and promised herself she wasn't going to have a tantrum over these events. She started to leave as he stopped her at the door. He invited her to stay for a drink. There was a heavy rain when Francesca decided to leave after drinking several glasses of wine. Damien indicated her reflexes weren't the best and insisted she stay the night since he didn't have to leave until the morning. She agreed and they went to bed. Damien approached her stating the weather was great for making love. She turned her back on him. Apparently annoyed, Damien turned his back on her rejection. Several hours passed and they were still unable to fall asleep.

Damien rolled over and looked towards Francesca's back, "If we had been making love all this time, we would have been asleep."

"Are you offering?" Francesca asked sarcastically.

"I was just making a statement. Francesca, sometimes a statement is just a statement!" Damien's serious tone had surprised her.

He finally fell asleep. Francesca quietly left his place without waking him. She arrived home safely. She soon was asleep in her warm bed with Dizzy at her feet. Her alarm sounded and she showered before going to work. During the day, she realized she should have been more understanding of a situation that wasn't in Damien's control. During the week, she would stay busy with the new project. She hoped the wait for his return to Atlanta wouldn't be long.

Another weekend was about to start without Francesca being with Damien. Friday night she arrived at her place with a surprise of roses on her porch. She picked them up and suddenly felt someone behind her. Francesca turned around quickly to be greeted by Damien. She embraced him and they entered her place with Damien immediately closing the door. He apologized for his absence and they continued a passionate embrace which led their desires being satisfied during the night. Saturday, they dined at her favorite bistro Giovanni's in the Vining's area then stayed at his place for the rest of the weekend. Monday morning, he kissed her as they left for their jobs.

After work Francesca called to thank Damien for a lovely weekend. He said he was going to relax and watch a preseason game of Monday Night Football. She thought she should return the favor of a surprise evening. Francesca picked up food and wine on her way to The Pointe. Since the guard wasn't there, she entered the code for the gate and drove up the hill. As she was turning the corner, she saw a tall attractive white female with long black hair in her thirties entering Damien's townhouse. Francesca wanted her surprise for him to be without an audience, so she parked her car in the next lot. She still had a view of his place but would wait until his visitor left. Time was passing slowly, and darkness was falling. She felt it was silly not to approach his door. But last time the surprise backfired on her with him preparing to leave town. Francesca decided to go to the pay phone by the clubhouse and call him. She knew she was probably jumping to the wrong conclusions about the situation. She heard his voice after several rings.

"Hello."

"Hello Damien. I was thinking about bringing you some food and wine so you could relax during the football game."

"Oh, that would be nice but I'm still really tired from traveling and this past weekend. Let me take a rain check on that."

"Fine. I'll talk to you later," she hid her disappointment from Damien.

Francesca cried after she put down the receiver. Should she drive back up the hill and confront him with Miss Monday Night Football or act like nothing happened? She didn't want to seem like Glenn Close out of "Fatal Attraction" but maybe this woman left when she went to make the call. Except for Tina, Francesca had never been jealous of him around any other woman. She was about to leave The Pointe when her pager started beeping. Damien's number appeared on the screen.

CHAPTER
FIFTEEN

It had been several days since Damien had returned from his father's party and she had once again received her apologetic bouquet of flowers. Francesca knew she should probably be more skeptical of his actions, but she loved him. Damien had assisted with the contract from his job. He didn't have to set it up. She was looking forward to seeing him and anxious to give him her gifts. Traffic was smooth as she made it in record time to The Pointe. Damien greeted her with a kiss. She handed him the packages and put the cake on the table. They sat on his sofa as she observed his satisfied expression while opening the gifts. Damien stated he loved the movies "Sleepless in Seattle" and "Casablanca." He gave her a kiss of appreciation. Tears started running down her cheeks. It saddened her that she couldn't spend his actual birthday with him since he would be out of town. Francesca wasn't sure how many more of these moments she would be sharing with him. Damien embraced Francesca to console her sorrow. She was able to compose herself as not to ruin his celebration. They enjoyed a glass of wine. She got up and prepared the slices of his red velvet birthday cake for them. Francesca decided to make this evening as adventurous as Damien had for her birthday. First, she took the fork and fed him the cake. Francesca took her silk scarf off from around her neck and proceeded to blindfold him. She ran to the freezer and retrieved a bowl of french vanilla ice cream. Soon she was unbuttoning his shirt while she had pushed him on his back. Her hand dropped a scoop of ice cream on his chest. Her attempts to stop the flow seemed futile as his warm body melted the frozen mass. She was captivated by his well chiseled body as her desire to please him intensified. Her kisses on his muscular upper region as she vacuumed up the sweetness from the ice cream made Damien roar with sounds of satisfaction. He appeared to have reached his limit when Damien grabbed Francesca and led her to the carpeted floor. His rapture brought her to a euphoric state. Eventually, they went upstairs to sleep exhausted after completion of their seduction towards each other.

The week had gone by fast as Francesca was preparing to leave the office Friday. She received the phone call she had dreamt would come true. When she hung up the phone she had to decide when to inform Damien of her news. He had made plans to cook her dinner and she didn't want to be late. Francesca rushed while traveling on I-20 westbound. Within fifteen minutes she was at- The Pointe. Damien opened the door. He offered her a drink as he took her coat. When he returned from the kitchen, she couldn't help but notice he was wearing the same outfit as the first day they had met. Damien leaned over to kiss her. He led her to the table which had candlelight and Italian food. She loved that he was being romantic by duplicating the elements of their first date. Perhaps this would be the perfect night to give her news. Maybe this meant he was going to ask her the question she had yearned to hear.

After dinner, he serenaded her with his sax accompanying her favorite jazz vocals in the background. He rekindled her desires as if it was their first intimate experience together. Francesca was filled with contentment looking into Damien's eyes before falling asleep. Morning came, Francesca opened her eyes to the sight of Damien's stare from the foot of the bed. He looked serious and was dressed in his shorts. She thought maybe she had slept through a phone call delivering bad news. He stated they needed to talk.

"This isn't easy for me, but we can't be intimate anymore," Damien's tone was calm.

Don't Judge A Book

"What are you talking about? What about the events you orchestrated last night?" Francesca's hostile response didn't appear to phase Damien.

"You know my situation. We can't keep doing this. I wanted our last time to be memorable for both of us," he attempted to justify his actions.

"You could have let me in on this master plan of yours and given me the option. Strike that, you were aware of how I feel about you and that I would have given in to you," she sternly replied.

"I'm sorry if you feel that I manipulated you, but it wasn't intentional," Damien tried to convince her.

"I guess there is nothing else to say at this point. Give me a few moments to get cleaned up and I'll be out of here." Francesca's disillusionment towards the situation was obvious.

Damien left the room; it gave her privacy. Francesca quickly jumped up from the bed then the room began to spin. She grabbed the side of the bed as she passed out on the floor. A few moments later, she awoke in Damien's arms as he was putting her on the bed.

He ran to the bathroom and returned with a cool wet cloth which he used to gently stroke her face. Francesca informed him she was feeling queasy and it was probably a hangover. He felt her forehead. Damien took her temperature. She had a fever of 102 degrees. She requested he give her a little time to compose herself. He insisted that she stay in bed. Damien showed compassion towards Francesca as he offered to care for her. Francesca felt too weak to argue even though her instincts wanted to be away from him after his initial morning rejection. Once she felt better, she could return to her place. She knew this wasn't the time to share her surprise.

CHAPTER
SIXTEEN

Francesca glared at the screen and decided he would be suspicious if she didn't respond to the page. She found more change and went back to the phone to call him. Damien said he had reconsidered her offer. Francesca stated she would be there in a few minutes since she was in the area. After ending the conversation, she realized he hadn't questioned her location. Hopefully, he assumed she was coming from Keisha's place. Francesca waited ten minutes then drove to the townhouse. Damien was waiting for her outside. He helped carry the dinner inside. She stated she felt the food needed to be hotter. Immediately, she warmed it up since it was almost cold. She was thankful he hadn't suspected her movements of the evening. Francesca felt foolish being jealous of Damien's actions. The game ended late with Francesca falling asleep on the sofa. Damien carried her into the bedroom for the night.

Several days had past and Francesca was excepting Damien for dinner. This was an anxious time for her since he would be meeting her father the next day. Damien arrived with his change of clothing. He carefully put them in her closet. Francesca reminded him that Dr. Stefani's ETA was ten in the morning. She emphasized they had to be dressed. Her father's words to her had been "I don't to walk into any surprises!" They enjoyed a quiet dinner and went to sleep early.

Morning came with Damien waking Francesca to the pleasant aroma of his cologne surrounding her body. They were soon oblivious to the sounds of the outside world that included the alarm. Suddenly, the doorbell rang several times. Francesca looked at the clock. Her level of distress rose as she realized her father must be at the door. In her frenzy, she jumped up while putting her clothes on as she pushed Damien into the bathroom to dress. She pulled her hair back in a bun attempting to try to act casual as she opened the door. Dr. Frank Stefani was a distinguished looking sixty-year-old with a slight tan. Francesca greeted him with a hug. She apologized for the delay in answering the door. Her father gave her a look of disbelief when he heard the bathroom door open and Damien entered the living room. She completed the introductions. She tried to ease the tense atmosphere by offering coffee. Francesca returned to the living room with the beverages. Dr. Stefani's reserved manner towards Damien seemed to mellow as they spoke over the next couple of hours. Damien excused himself before saying goodbye to them. She stated Damien had errands to run but would be meeting them later for dinner. Her father still seemed leery of her new lover but had never interfered in the past. They soon left to meet Brian for lunch in The Underground. Francesca's pager buzzed. She excused herself to find a phone. When she returned, she announced Damien wouldn't be joining them for dinner. Unfortunately, he had to tend to his injured brother out of town. He would call later with an update. Brian made no comment, but it was apparent from his expression he wasn't surprised by the news of another cancellation from Damien. Francesca tried to keep occupied during the rest of the weekend with her father without discussion of her current love life. Dr. Stefani left late Sunday afternoon. His only advice was to be cautious in her life choices. Before she went to bed Damien called giving a favorable update on his brother's condition.

Wednesday night she arrived at the Peters' house for dinner. Brian was already sitting in the living room. She hadn't seen much of them since her involvement with Damien. During the evening nobody inquired about Damien. She assumed Brian had informed them of the latest events with her father's dinner. Francesca respected their opinions, but this was one subject they would agree to disagree. At the end of the evening Brian escorted Francesca outside. She was tempted to give the update on Damien's brother proving it was a legitimate reason for his absence. Instead, she gave him a hug at her car.

Damien had returned from his trip. He said he had some big news from work to share with her. They made plans to see each other that night. Francesca thought it must be a promotion allowing him to feel more confident about making their relationship permanent. Francesca rushed to The Pointe. She anxiously knocked on his door. Damien opened it. He guided her to the sofa. He looked more serious than usual. His chest rose as he took a deep breath and made the statement.

"My company has informed me they need me to move back to Charleston. It won't be for several months, but I needed to tell you." Damien was addressing these new facts in a business tone.

"Isn't there any way you can turn them down and stay in Atlanta? Don't you have a choice?" Francesca's astonishment couldn't be suppressed.

"It would be a promotion and I think it would be the best move for my career," Damien continued in his calm tone.

"What am I supposed to say? Let me think a minute," she paused for a moment. "This isn't the end of the world. I'll be graduating at the end of the semester and can apply for a job in Charleston. Would you have a problem with that?" Francesca's eagerness to resolve their logistical issue in her mind was plausible.

"No, I wouldn't have a problem with that. Charleston is a big area. But make sure that's the best move for your career. I don't think you understand what I'm saying to you. I'm not asking for marriage," Damien was pursuing to make his opinion clear to her.

"What do you mean? What's not to understand, you're moving to Charleston and you weren't sure if I would do the same without a ring. Right?" Francesca's naïve response was sincere.

"No, I'm moving and feel we should end it immediately. I've enjoyed our time together and think it would be easier for us to call it quits." Damien's adamant reaction shocked Francesca.

"Why can't you consider my alternative plan? We don't have to be engaged or living together. You have given our relationship chances in the past. What's different?" Francesca felt baffled over his decision.

"I just don't want to mislead you in a possible long-term future with me," Damien returned to his calm tone.

"I'll miss you and probably always continue to love you." Francesca was hoping stating her feelings would change his mind.

"You'll get over me," he laughed. "Remember, you can always place another ad in the Personals!" Damien flippantly responded.

Devastated, Francesca cried hysterically as Damien attempted a remorseful apology for the hurtful statement. He said he was trying to ease the tension but didn't mean to be cruel to her. She gathered her purse while heading for the door. Damien grabbed her saying he couldn't let her leave until she was calmer. He guided her back to the sofa. She was soon in his embrace. He wiped the tears from her face then gave her a gentle kiss which turned into a passionate one. Francesca felt herself being swept away by his soothing actions. The next morning before leaving she gave him a kiss without waking him.

CHAPTER SEVENTEEN

Saturday night Francesca sat in the armchair clutching her glass of wine while aimlessly staring at Keisha passed out on the sofa, and Keisha's brother, Tyrone asleep on the other armchair. Her instincts were to get out of Keisha's place and into her warm bed. She knew her drinking had become a problem again. But it was her only escape from the pain she felt from Damien's recent rejection. Her drinking binge had to stop. She stood up with her glass of wine to start towards the kitchen. Her unsteadiness caused her to stumble spilling the red wine on her white sweater and the carpet. She dropped to her knees and began to cry softly.

Francesca pulled herself up from a crawling position. She went to the kitchen to frantically search for cleaning materials. Francesca returned to the living room. Her attempt to remove the wine stain from the carpet was fairly successful. Her face began to feel flushed, she thought the fresh air would help her current condition. Loudly her hand opened the sliding glass door to the patio. The cold winter breeze was a shock to her system. Quickly she slammed the door. Luckily, the sounds hadn't disturbed either Keisha or Tyrone.

Francesca grabbed her coat from the armchair then searched for the keys in her purse. She convinced herself that the cold breeze would sober her up. Francesca boldly opened the front door of the second-floor condo to the outside then her hand gripped the railing. She tried to keep her balance descending on the stairs as she finally reached her car. Her body was uncontrollably shivering as she waited for her car to warm up. Her Mustang appeared to stay in the lane while making the few curves on the level surface. Francesca had the challenge of maneuvering the winding curves up the hill to exit The Woodlands, which appeared to be a ninety-degree angle. She used a death grip on the steering wheel. The car ventured over the white line several times before she reached the stop sign. Thankfully, there was no oncoming traffic. The right turn onto South Cobb Drive was clear as she quickly gunned the acceleration pedal. Her stomach felt as though it would enter her chest as the car zoomed on the roller coaster dip towards the Cumberland Parkway intersection light. Suddenly, she heard the blaring sound of a horn while her car zigzagged in and out of lanes. Francesca's reflexes were no longer in her control. She would never make it home alive if she continued towards The Perimeter Parkway for her Midtown destination. The light changed forcing her to make a possible risky decision. She was so close to his place. Within a block on the right, she saw the front gate of The Pointe. She pulled in the parking lot. Francesca slammed on the brakes when she approached the clubhouse. She stumbled out of her car onto the sidewalk to use the phone. She slowly picked up the receiver, deposited the coins from her purse, and began dialing. Her hands trembled as she waited for the voice on the other end while her heart was beating rapidly.

"Hello," Damien said in a sleepy voice.

"Hello Damien," she responded trying not to slur her words.

"It's three in the morning!" Damien responded in an exasperated tone.

"I'm sorry for the hour but if I wasn't desperate, I wouldn't have called you. I've been drinking at Keisha's place. I didn't think I could drive home safely. Please let me sleep on your sofa tonight!" Francesca nervously replied.

"Doesn't Keisha have a sofa? Why can't you stay at her place?" Damien sarcastically responded.

"Her brother was visiting and there wasn't any place for me to sleep. I won't bother you anymore. Just please do this favor for me!" Francesca pleaded.

"Where are you?" Damien asked.

"I'm at the clubhouse at the pay phone." She was hopeful he would allow her to stay.

"Alright but this is the last time. Do you want me to come and get you?" His firm tone alarmed her.

"No, I'll leave my car at the clubhouse. I need to walk some of this wine off," she tried to continue speaking clearly.

"Alright, I'll see you in a few minutes," Damien quickly hung up.

Francesca returned to her car and attempted to park it properly then locked it. She was amazed she was able to navigate his gate code to enter the complex. After numerous falls on the massive incline, she finally made it to Damien's place. Francesca knocked on his door. He opened it wearing only his white terry cloth running shorts. She immediately ran past him to the bathroom. She felt the need to throw-up or pass out but neither happened. When she exited the master bathroom, she saw Damien lying on his bed with the comforter snuggled around his body. Francesca stood at the foot of his bed.

"Thank you, Damien. I really appreciate this. Good night."

After no response was heard she felt his rejection once again. Tears began to slowly roll down her cheeks. She then went downstairs unsteadily into the living room. There was a pillow and blanket on the sofa. Francesca sloppily prepared the bedding for the sofa when she saw the Panther's jersey on the coffee table. She had always loved his jersey with the scent of Cool Water remembering the past times she had worn it to bed. But this time she wouldn't be sleeping with Damien nor be pleasantly awoken by him removing the jersey from her body before one of their memorable lovemaking sessions. Francesca took off her wine-stained sweater replacing it with the jersey. Her clothing was removed, they dropped into a messy pile on the floor. Her head began to throb massively as she attempted to get comfortable on the sofa. Suddenly Francesca bolted from the sofa and raced upstairs to the master bathroom stumbling past Damien's bed. She began to rid her system of the Zinfandel. Approximately thirty minutes later she could hear a knock on the door.

"Francesca, are you alright?" His tone showed concern.

"No," she responded trying to hold back the tears.

"Do you need help? I'm coming in!" He professed his intent before the door opened. Damien glared at her with a look of disgust as she knelt beside the toilet.

"I'm sorry I'm so sick and kept you up." She felt his disappointment in her.

"Why are you doing this? What made you go back to drinking?" The anger in his voice scared her and she started crying profusely.

"I do this to numb the pain. I can live without drinking. I can't live with this pain!" Francesca tried to defend her actions.

Damien's eyes turned from anger to sadness as he approached her, "Let me help you up so you can freshen up."

"Please let me sleep in the bed with you. I won't bother you. I can't fall asleep on the sofa, I tried!" She realized her request probably seemed pathetic to him.

Damien picked up Francesca from the floor and carried her to his bed. He laid her down then tucked in the comforter. Damien walked to the other side and crawled in next to her. He turned his back to her as she tried to become comfortable. Luckily, she no longer felt queasy or dizzy. Nearly an hour had passed without either of them being able to fall asleep.

"Do you want to lie on my chest?" Damien whispered.

Francesca rolled to face him. She was stunned by his offer but happy to have the opportunity to return to a familiar position with Damien.

"Yes, thank you," she responded in a soft voice. After she positioned herself on his chest she looked up towards his face. "I'm sorry for all the trouble I've caused in your life. I'll probably always love you. I hope you find the happiness you're looking for in your life. I love you."

Francesca waited for a few minutes for his response, but none came. She then dropped her head back down on his chest and her crying resumed. The moisture of her tears poured on his chest. He then slowly pressed his warm lips on her forehead giving her a gentle good night kiss. Serenity radiated throughout Francesca's body. The emotional chaos of the night had exhausted her. She had felt this feeling before. Her relationship with Damien was going to be once again calm, at least for that moment she thought. Damien murmured good night to her. Francesca's eyes finally closed as she fell asleep in his protective arms.

Daylight seemed to arrive quickly. The sun peeked through the blinds shining on Francesca's face. She began to stretch onto her back. Her arm felt for his presence but there was only an empty space. Francesca's eyes opened as she jolted from the bed. Frantically she looked through the townhouse her eyes stopped, she saw Damien's tall muscular body curled up on the sofa. Her eyes filled with tears as she thought of the love they had once shared.

Francesca quickly put her clothes on, as flashbacks of their memorable lovemaking, their baby's death, and Damien's probable infidelity with Tina entered her mind. She had once thought love was the belief that the person you loved always must be truthful. But mostly they would never betray or leave you. Damien was going to leave her.

In the future, she would never show her true emotions to someone she cared about. If they parted, she'll hurt for a short time instead of a lifetime feeling pain and a void which can never be filled with real happiness again. Francesca grabbed her belongings and rushed towards the front door. She hesitated briefly as she passed the sofa. As the tears continued to rush down her face, she then realized his love for her was just a memory. Francesca bent over and gave Damien a gentle goodbye kiss on his cheek. She then paused to take one last glance at his motionless body before she exited his life.

CHAPTER EIGHTEEN

Francesca tried to concentrate on her new project at work. Luckily, she had finished the assignment with Damien's company and wouldn't have to deal with the possibility of running into him at his job. She had spoken to Brian during the day but had quickly ended the conversation when he inquired about her last date with Damien. It was close to quitting time and the receptionist informed her she had a visitor. Francesca was surprised to see Brian in the lobby. They used to get together for lunch often when she was attending her classes at Georgia State University near Woodruff Park. Brian's job was nearby at Peachtree Center. She loved the gothic style skyscraper where his law firm was housed. She missed those moments with him. He stated he was coming back from doing research at Emory Law Library and needed a dinner with his sister. She knew he was checking up on her. Francesca loved his big-hearted manner.

They went to his favorite restaurant in The Underground. Mikki's was a three-level establishment. Two of the levels were restaurants with the top level being a dance club. They chose to enter the lower more elegant half. After being seated, Brian immediately demanded the details of what Damien had done to her. Her voice began choking up as she described the events of their last encounter. Brian attentively listened and held her hand as she displayed the look of heartbreak on her face. She ended by telling Brian her alternative solution and that she wasn't sure if it was over since they were intimate. Francesca gave a detailed explanation of her job search for the Charleston area. She had sent out resumes to St. Francis Hospital, Naval Hospital, and Medical University of South Carolina. Even if the relationship with Damien was over, she felt she needed a change of environment. Living by a beach would refresh her outlook on life. She felt it was probably hard for Brian not to give his usual advice. She needed a sounding board and he kept silent. The remainder of the dinner was quiet. Brian escorted Francesca home. She thanked him for his caring actions before saying goodnight.

Several days had passed when she found an envelope on her front porch. She entered her place and began to shake as she read the note, "You will pay for what has been done to me!" There was an article attached to it about a victim of a hit and run incident. Francesca couldn't imagine who would send her such threats! Her first reaction was to call Damien, but she stopped herself. She jumped as the phone rang. Francesca was relieved to hear Kenny's voice. He wanted to sleep on her sofa for the night since they were fumigating his place. She agreed since she was thankful for the protection of a strong male unsure if the note was a sick practical joke or not.

Kenny arrived within the hour bringing take-out for them. He questioned her about what was upsetting her. She decided to let him read the note with a promise of not informing Brian. Kenny hesitantly agreed but wanted to discuss the possible author of the note. Francesca couldn't think of anyone. He pressed the issue of Damien or his associates but except for Tina, who was unaware of her existence, she didn't think that was a possibility. Kenny did mention the name of Eddie Sloane. Francesca was shocked that he would dare to mention that name to her. Eddie was a twenty-one-year-old black man with a muscular built, as she found out the hard way, he had a violent streak in him. Luckily, she had only had a brief fling with him years ago. The last time she heard about him was when she was interrogated by the police, she had informed them of his latest hangouts. They had a warrant for his arrest due to an auto theft ring he had masterminded. Francesca was surprised that Eddie had turned out to be a criminal but that was during her rebound period after her divorce. She hadn't heard anything about Eddie recently, so she dismissed both of Kenny's theories. Francesca thanked Kenny for his concern, but the note was probably just a practical joke since it didn't have her name on it. She changed the subject as they continued their dinner. Kenny was a true example of an Omega Man. He always displayed the Four Cardinal Principles: Manhood, Perseverance, Uplift, and Scholarship. She loved his moral character and willingness to go the extra mile for his friends. Sometimes she wished Damien would be more like Kenny. Too bad our hearts don't have a brain that could control who or when we fall in love. It was getting late when she said goodnight to Kenny.

The next morning Francesca was in the shower when the phone rang. Kenny awoke from a deep sleep as he answered the phone. The male voice on the other end asked to speak to Francesca. Kenny informed the caller she was unavailable and did they want to leave a message. Francesca soon entered the room in her robe when she saw Kenny on the phone. Kenny told the caller to wait a moment. He handed the phone to Francesca. She answered with a pleasant hello and Damien immediately grilled her about who was at her place this hour of the morning. She informed him it was Kenny and it really didn't concern him anymore. Francesca then asked the reason for his call. Damien stated he couldn't find his jersey, and did she have it? She replied she didn't think it was at her place, but she would call if it turned up. He said he would appreciate it before he said goodbye. Francesca hung up the phone. She apologized to Kenny if Damien was rude to him. Kenny stated he didn't want to pry but if she wanted to vent, nothing would go beyond these four walls. She said she wasn't in the mood to get into it at this time.

Kenny took a shower as Francesca finished dressing in her bedroom. She was gathering her laundry when she saw Damien's jersey on the floor of her closet. Kenny was dressed as he came out of the bathroom. She quickly threw the jersey down before she escorted him to the other room. He thanked her as he kissed her goodbye on her cheek.

Francesca was going to call Damien but decided against it. She went to her bedroom then grabbed the jersey before she left for The Pointe. Since it was Saturday, she knew he was a fanatic about his errands, and she could leave it at the front door in a bag. Francesca wouldn't have to confront him if she timed it right. She didn't see his car as she pulled into a parking space. Francesca walked to his front door and was about to put the bag on the doorknob as it suddenly opened. She was startled to see Damien in the entrance.

"What are you doing here?" He looked surprised.

"I found your jersey and was returning it," Francesca's tone was stern.

"You weren't going to ring the bell but instead sneak away?" Damien questioned her actions.

"I thought you weren't home since I didn't see your car. I was going to leave it in a bag on the doorknob," Francesca responded anxiously.

"My car is in the shop for maintenance and I have a rental. You could have called me. I would have come to your place to pick it up." Damien attempted to show his willingness to be civil towards the situation.

"I knew you were anxious to have your jersey, at least that's what you told me on the phone," she said sarcastically.

"Can we discuss this privately inside?" Damien responded.

"I just wanted to give you the jersey. I did that. I'm leaving. Goodbye and have a nice life!" Francesca scowled.

"Francesca, please come inside and let's have a conversation."

Francesca had felt the need to have control of the conversation. "I'm not in the mood for another grilling like this morning on the phone. I hope you weren't rude to my friend."

"I want to apologize for my behavior on the phone. Can we finish this inside?" Damien's urgency to change location was apparent.

"It's against my better judgement but I guess I can spare you some time," Francesca conceded.

"Thank you!" He escorted her into his place, and they sat on the sofa.

Francesca's anger could not be hidden. "What was the urgency of me coming inside? I think you were clear with your wishes the last time I was here. I only have one question. Was that last bit of intimacy between us, was it pity or just for the hell of it?"

"It wasn't for either. I still care about your feelings and didn't want to see you upset. I'm still attracted to you and things just happened between us," Damien's reassuring tone always made her calm.

Damien looked deep into her eyes as he gave her an everlasting kiss. Francesca yearned for his presence to intertwine with hers one more time. Her mind tried to resist the temptation, but her body couldn't. The weakness of her desires finally gave in as he slowly removed his shirt. The exhilaration of their actions soon consumed the day as sunset had arrived. As the room became darker, they realized they hadn't eaten all day. Damien put on his robe and went to the kitchen. Francesca put on his jersey then joined him. He made them cheese omelets and prepared strawberries on the side. She was feeling tranquil until Damien brought up the subject of Kenny.

"Why was he at your place so early this morning?" His tone was serious.

"He spent the night on the sofa since his place was being fumigated," Francesca quickly answered.

"Why didn't he stay with Brian?" Damien continued the questioning.

"Brian was out of town and wasn't going to be back until tomorrow. What's the problem? I was helping a friend," Francesca responded innocently.

"I don't like you spending that much time with a former lover!" Damien's accusatory manner surprised her.

"You spend time with Tina, but I can't have a strictly platonic friendship with Kenny? What a double standard!" Her defiant statement incited an immediate response from Damien.

"I explained the situation with Tina and how she sometimes needs extra help with the boys. And I feel responsible for her accident." He affirmed his reasons to her.

"Are you going back to her in Charleston?" She was hoping he would deny her question.

"I told you my job is sending me back to Charleston!" Damien was adamant.

"I thought today meant we were back together." Francesca wanted validation that she had made the right decision for her future.

"No, it meant we had another memorable time together," he bluntly responded.

"Great, I keep giving myself to you and letting you deep into my soul. I don't need this from you. I have enough drama in my life with the uncertainty of who is threatening me!" She was showing her high anxiety level.

"What are you talking about? Who is threatening you?" Damien appeared to show concern.

"Oh, why you care?" Her sarcasm was apparent.

He demanded, "Francesca, please tell me what is going on?"

Francesca yelled at him, "The note said I'll pay for what has been done to this person. I haven't a clue who sent it. When Kenny called, I was scared and thankful to have protection in the house for the night. Any more questions?"

"I'm sorry. Did you call Brian? He'd probably have contacts that could investigate the threat." Damien stated compassionately.

"No, I don't want to involve anyone-else. I'm hoping it is a sick practical joke and go away. I shouldn't have told you since we are no longer together." She was no longer yelling, and her tone was calmer.

"I still care if someone is threatening you. I wish you would call Brian." Damien stood up from the table and started towards the bedroom.

"Where are you going?" She inquired.

"I'm not going to fight anymore," he said in a nonchalant manner.

"Good. I win!" She felt she had won a victory.

"You can fight all you want but I'm going to sleep. Goodnight, Francesca," his facial expression showed no emotion.

"God, that drives me nuts about you," Francesca's frustration level was obvious.

"It is wasted energy to fight or be mad," Damien stated calmly.

"Can we have a cease fire?" she wanted confirmation.

"Sure, I'm going to bed. You can stay if you want. I don't care."

Damien went upstairs then shut the door to his bedroom. Francesca stayed in the living room to gather her clothes. She decided if he wanted his space, she would give it to him. Francesca took off his Panthers jersey then put her clothes on. She quickly exited the townhouse and screeched the wheels of her car out of the parking lot. Francesca arrived home. She tried to get sleep due to her hospital shift the next day.

The next day during her shift she was reflecting on the staff who had taught her numerous techniques she would always remember. Francesca was down to the home stretch with a few months to go fulfilling her requirements during her, Signature Experience. She would mainly miss her supervisor, Dr. Scott Barber. He was a white male in his mid-fifties that was almost a foot taller than her. His mannerisms reminded her of her father. Francesca was assigned to evaluate a new patient, John Pierce. John was a white male in his early twenties with a large physique. He was brought in earlier by his sister. She stated he had stopped taking his medications for depression. At the moment he was calm while he sat quietly in the wheelchair in the examination area. Francesca introduced herself and attempted to confirm his name. John started bellowing his response, "No!" as he lunged at her from the wheelchair. Francesca shrieked "Stop!" as she jumped back and barely moved enough so she wouldn't hit the wall.

CHAPTER
NINETEEN

It had been weeks since Francesca had seen Damien. She thought when she exited his townhouse after her drinking incident, she could continue her life without him. But due to the recent series of events that wouldn't be possible. Francesca had wanted to tell him about her job offer in Charleston the night of their last romantic encounter. However, his announcement of finally ending their relationship had stopped her. She wasn't sure with this new development how she would approach him. Francesca couldn't believe she was pregnant again. After her miscarriage, the doctor informed her the chances of conceiving were low. Maybe this was a blessing in disguise for her to finally achieve motherhood. Damien had told her he wouldn't mind if she moved to Charleston. Since her attack they had been getting closer until recently. Francesca was glad she had pursued her alternative plan. She was excited about her new job in Charleston. Francesca felt before the move her conscious needed to be clear of secrets. She contemplated how to reveal these revelations to Damien of their impending parenthood and her Medical University of South Carolina, (MUSC) job.

Her phone rang. She was surprised it was the police. The detective stated Eddie Sloane had been arrested and was responsible for her attack. She was astonished but Kenny had suggested he may be the one. After she finished her conversation with the police, she immediately called Damien. She hoped he would be relieved with the arrest. This was a good reason to start a conversation with him. Francesca waited patiently as she rehearsed her lines.

"Hello," Damien answered in a monotone voice.

"Hello Damien. Did I catch you at a bad time?" she tried to state in a low-key manner.

"Actually, I'm in the middle of something. What do you want?" Damien abruptly responded.

"I thought you might be interested that the police arrested someone for my attack," Francesca tried to overlook his negative tone.

162

"Who was it?" he asked.

"Unfortunately, it was someone from my past. But that was over long before I met you." She wanted to reassure him that she had always been faithful during their relationship.

"Well, I'm glad it worked out safely for you. I have to go," he responded expeditiously.

"I really need to see you before you move," Francesca attempted to appeal to him.

"I can't have this conversation. I told you I'm busy but it's like you never have listened to me or you don't care!" Damien's berated tone shocked her.

"That's not true. I just want to set a time to see you. Why can't we see each other again? Are you afraid you may be seduced or something?" her defensive and satirical manner was demonstrated.

"We are past that stage of our relationship," his sarcasm could be heard.

163

"I never thought you would be cruel. I'm sure you used to love me. Otherwise, you wouldn't have assisted with my recovery from the attack or car accident. What did I ever do to you?"

"Nothing, it's not you it's me," Damien flippantly replied.

"I don't understand. Is it Tina? You told me at the beginning she wanted you to move and get back together," Francesca's inquiring mind needed to be satisfied.

"I never said the relationship between Tina, and I had been bad," Damien harshly responded as her relentless questions seemed to agitate him.

"It hasn't been only me calling you. You did call me over the holidays," She was affirming.

"I only called you once after we stopped seeing each other. I told you I have to go," he vigorously retorted.

Before Francesca responded Damien had hung up on her. She knew it was over between them. However, she felt he had a right to be told about the baby. Francesca had to deliver this news in person since this attempt had failed. Damien wouldn't be responsive tonight. She would wait until her final clinical shift was over on Sunday.

The day finally came for her to give goodbyes to her co-workers at the hospital. Towards the end of her shift, they surprised her with a party. Dr. Barber had given her a glowing reference to her new employer. She gave her final parting to Dr. Barber as he sent her off with well wishes. She took her last walk to the Georgia Baptist Hospital garage to her car. Her emotions were bittersweet as she ended this chapter of her life.

Francesca drove towards The Pointe and decided she wouldn't be emotional when she saw him. Soon she had arrived then parked her car. Several deep breaths had to be taken as she walked to his townhouse. Her hand knocked on his door. Several minutes past with no response. A car pulled up next to her car. She recognized one of his neighbors. The lady said hello to Francesca and informed her that Damien had moved out yesterday with his family helping him. Francesca thanked the neighbor for her assistance. Suspended in time, she was disoriented. Her body wasn't sure whether to go to her car or sit down at Damien's former front door to cry. Francesca felt the need for affirmation. She rushed to peek through his opened blinds and saw the bare townhouse.

CHAPTER TWENTY

Francesca thought back on Damien's words that he only called her once during the Thanksgiving holiday. He was right. Had she become so codependent on him that her reality of events had become distorted? Her mind was on happier times since she had completed the December graduation ceremony with her parents and friends in attendance including Angie. She was happy Angie had been able to make the trip. Brian and Angie were the only ones who were aware of Francesca's condition. It was getting difficult to hide her symptoms since her morning sickness had turned into whenever sickness. She was kidding herself if she thought her father the doctor hadn't figured it out. However, he was respecting her privacy and hadn't confronted her on the issue. Her parents only stayed a few days before they returned home. Everyone had shown support in Francesca's decision to accept the excellent position with the Medical University of South Carolina. Her new employer had been informed of her pending motherhood. Brian, Kenny, Julie, and Ron had offered to help her move. This would be her last Christmas living

167

in Atlanta. She had already found a small house rental in the North area of Charleston. Kenny was going to keep an eye on her place in Atlanta until her lease was expired. Brian had offered to keep Dizzy. Finally, things were falling into place.

It had sneaked up on her that tomorrow was moving day. Kenny had been at her place every evening to assist her with the packing. A couple times she had almost confided in him about Damien and the pregnancy. She felt it would be a bad decision since Kenny had always been protective of her. Kenny's feelings had been important to Francesca and these last moments in Atlanta she didn't want to upset him. Francesca was sad to leave her beautiful place next to Piedmont Park along with the memories it had for her over the years. She was starting a new life style and felt she could be a good mother. Damien's love for her was dead but she would always love their child. She awoke early to prepare for the trip. The group arrived within the hour and promptly had the moving van loaded. They had arranged to stop at the Cayce exit off I-26 eastbound near Columbia, South Carolina. The one truck and two car caravans began their adventure as they entered I-75 southbound from 10th Street. Kenny along with Brian were in the truck and Ron followed in his car. She was glad Julie was keeping her company. The traffic was at a snail's pace as they navigated through the Grady Curve and exited to I-20 eastbound.

Once they were past The Perimeter on the outskirts of Atlanta, traffic was smooth sailing until Augusta. Bright orange construction barriers were lining up the left lane as traffic was squeezing to the right. Francesca was concerned with Kenny maneuvering the truck but saw in her rearview mirror he seemed to do it with ease. Luckily, it was a gorgeous day. Right before the bridge the orange barriers disappeared. As they exited Georgia onto the bridge, she felt she was entering the promised land of South Carolina, free of traffic jams. Her and Julie admired the wooded scenery for the remainder of I-20. The winding merge of Exit 64 onto I-26 eastbound made Francesca queasy. She was glad their meeting place would be soon.

At the truck stop, Francesca dashed to the bathroom. She knelt beside the commode waiting for the eruption, but nothing submerged. After ten minutes she departed the stall and threw cold water on her face once she washed her hands. Francesca immediately popped a Phenergan which had become her new best friend. She was glad the feeling to throw-up passed and was able to return to her friends. Brian promptly offered to drive for her. She tried to blow it off to a case of the nerves. Kenny's look of disbelief registered a level of guilt in her. Maybe she had made the wrong decision in not sharing the news with him.

Soon they were back on the road with Francesca laying in the back seat fast asleep. Kenny was alone being a truck driver since as usual Brian had come to the rescue. She awoke and sat up to see the Summerville exit. Her excitement was increasing as they eventually made it to I-526 westbound towards her new home's exit. It took almost five hours for the arrival at her new place. They quickly had the rental truck unloaded and returned. She was grateful for the help since she couldn't do any heavy lifting.

They stayed at her place while they reminisced. In the middle of the night Brian woke up from the sofa to see Francesca sitting at the dining table. He approached her as he saw a troubled look on her face. He asked if he could help. She proceeded to tell him the details of Damien's last conversation and his disappearance from her life. Brian said if she was insistent on contacting him about the baby, he would help her. He went to his overnight bag. Soon he returned with a name and number. Brian stated a college friend of his from Emory University School of Law was a lawyer in Charleston and could track down Damien for her. He warned her that she better be prepared for a negative response when Damien gets the news since he was probably with Tina. Francesca agreed to accept the circumstances. The following morning Francesca thanked the merry group of four for moving her. They said their goodbyes as she waved tearfully to them.

The next day Francesca was tired from unpacking but had a couple of days to rest before her orientation for the new job. She called to set-up an appointment with Brian's lawyer friend, Mr. Sam Clark. Sam Clark had a cancellation that afternoon and gave her directions to his office. He told her that parking was likely going to be scarce on Broad Street and she should park in a public garage on Queen Street. Francesca was dressed in a loose fitting long sleeved blue dress she had recently bought in a size bigger than usual. She wanted to be able to wear it as long as possible with her pending weight gain. Her feet donned black flats in case the walk was farther than anticipated to his office.

Soon she was traveling on I-26 eastbound. The curves on the elevated overpass of the upper peninsula today weren't upsetting her stomach as she passed the East Bay/Morrison Drive exit. Remembering to take the exit to Meeting Street she merged left. The ramp declined as she made the right turn onto Meeting Street.

After passing Mary Street she saw the Visitor's Center which seemed to be a former train station. It appeared she had stepped into Colonial Times when she observed the amazing architectural designs of the churches at Marion Square and the historical fire station at Wentworth Street. At the light by The Market, she looked to the right to see The Shops at The Omni. Immediately, she thought about Damien's story of Tina's accident. Tears began rolling down her face as she wondered if it hadn't been for that incident maybe things would have been different with Damien.

She needed to clear her mind of these unrealistic images. She saw The Mill House Hotel and made the right onto Queen Street. The hotel was gorgeous with wrought iron balconies and the palmetto trees lined along the side of it. The parking garage was past Poogan's Porch Restaurant which was located in a house styled from several centuries ago. Luckily, there were open spaces in the garage, and she walked back to Queen Street. It felt as though she was in a different century walking towards King Street before making the left. The wind blew slightly but was pleasant for January. It was a relief not to wear a coat. She could understand why Damien loved this area. The final part of her journey was almost done as she passed Berlin's Clothing's old-fashioned blue sign to cross Broad Street. The law firm was in a Charleston Single House with a gable end facing the street and a longer second floor piazza facing a few parking spots. The yellowish tan painted house was a three story with the top being an attic. Below windows could be seen from the street to the basement. The black shutters pressed against the building made the white lined windows appear to have a clean look. The early 1800's house was connected to another historical structure. Francesca opened the white door ornate with lantern style lamps on each side. She found several steep steps when she climbed to the lower privacy porch then entered another door to the inside reception area and greeted by the receptionist.

Francesca was instructed that Mr. Clark would be with her momentarily. It wasn't long until a well-dressed white twenty-seven-year-old male with a tall slender stature and brown hair approached her. He introduced himself and she followed him into his office. Mr. Clark informed her he had received a call from Brian this morning regarding her situation. Francesca was relieved Brian had taken the initiative. Mr. Clark stated he had an investigator named Adam Sears on retainer. He said it shouldn't be hard to locate Damien since she knew his last address, employer, and the former girlfriend's name in Charleston. At the end of the meeting Mr. Clark said he would be in touch in a few days. Francesca hated that she had to be sneaky, but Damien hadn't left her any option.

She had been tense, during the meeting and her nerves were shot after memories of Damien kept reoccurring. Her mind needed to be cleared. Leaving the law firm, she decided to be touristy and explored the sights.

At the Four Corners of Law, she observed the beauty of St. Michael's Church. She loved that no structures on the peninsula could be higher than the steeple on top of it otherwise, it was thought you were trying to be above God. It amazed her as she went up Meeting Street nobody was rushing while walking or that horns weren't being honked especially around the horse drawn carriage rides. While walking she heard a local tour guide explain that to blow your car horn in Charleston was considered rude and meant your Mama didn't raise you right! It was going to be a change from the city life of Atlanta, but this calmer lifestyle would be good to raise a child.

During the rest of the week Francesca was settling into her new life. On Saturday morning, she received a call from Mr. Sears requesting a meeting with her. He suggested it might be in her best interest not to meet in public. Francesca gave him directions to her house, and he agreed to be there at two. She was nervous what details Mr. Sears had found out that needed to be delivered in private. The doorbell rang promptly at two. Francesca opened the door to a thirty-eight-year-old white male that was over six feet tall with blonde hair.

"Hello, my name is Francesca Stefani, but you can call me Francesca," she extended her hand.

"It's nice to meet you. My name is Adam Sears, and you can call me Adam." he reciprocated with his hand.

"Please come in. Let's sit at the table," Francesca guided him to the dining area.

"Thank you. Tell me your story about Damien Sommers," Adam was straightforward.

"We practically lived together in Atlanta. He had an ex-girlfriend named Tina Perez in Charleston. His job transferred to Atlanta then back to Charleston suddenly." Her bewilderment in Damien's life was evident.

"I've been advised about your condition and there is no easy way to give you this news," Adam paused.

"What is it? Is he a criminal or something?" Francesca asked anxiously.

"You'll probably feel he is after I tell you the whole story. Are you sure you are up for this?" Adam hesitated.

"Just tell me everything at once and don't spare me any details," she pleaded.

"His name is Damien Sommers, and he is in a management position for a national company. But his employer sent him to Atlanta for a year assignment to set-up a new division. According to my sources, Mr. Sommers knew it was only temporary and he would be able to return to the Charleston office. Mr. Sommers currently resides in an older exclusive northern area near The Woodlands Inn, a historical resort built in the early 1900's, with his wife of three years, Tina Perez Sommers and her two sons from a previous marriage. They live in a million-dollar house and it is in Tina Perez's name. Over the past year he had been making trips to visit his family in Charleston. Mr. Sommers' brothers are lawyers, and his father is a judge. His mother died of cancer when he was a child. Are you ready for the last part?" Adam appeared to be considerate of her feelings as he waited for her response.

"There's more? How much worse can it get?" Francesca could barely speak.

"His family is well respected in the church community. On the weekends, Mr. Sommers is Deacon Sommers in the First Baptist Church. Apparently, he took a leave of absence during his stay in Atlanta but has returned to the pulpit." He stopped and there was a silence.

"Are you sure?" she whispered.

"Do you want to see the photos?" Adam showed an envelope to her.

"Show them to me!" Francesca gained her composure.

Francesca looked at the photos of Damien. He was in front of a three-story red brick Colonial style house. The top level had two bay style windows protruding from the roof bordered with a white paint. The second and first floor windows reminded her of Mr. Clark's law firm with the black shutters highlighted by white. There was a great white arch for the main door bordered with beveled glass on each side. The driveway in front of the house was a half-

177

moon for an easy entrance and exit. She noticed there was a small guest house to the side of the main house with its own driveway. The yard had well-manicured shrubs and a great oak tree in front. The final photo was an older Hispanic woman standing near him leaning on a cane. She couldn't help but notice the age difference between Damien and Tina. At least he hadn't lied about her injuries or the kids. Thinking back, she realized the gold band with the diamond in it was his wedding ring and he had only switched it to the right hand. Francesca's whole world surrounding Damien had been a mirage deceitfully maneuvered by him. She didn't want to break down in front of Adam, who was a stranger to her. Francesca held back the tears and continued her questions.

"How old is Tina? Does she work?" her voice was shaking.

"She is ten-years older than Mr. Sommers. Due to her accident and inheritance from her first husband's death, she wasn't employed. How do you want to proceed with this case?" Adam patiently replied.

"This has overwhelmed me. I have to take some time to absorb this information. I can't personally notify him at home. I would hate to ruin Tina's life with the news of her husband's double life and pending fatherhood." Francesca's look of mental exhaustion was obvious.

"When you're ready I can contact him discreetly away from his family. Take your time." Adam suggested as he stood up and headed towards the door.

"Thank you for your help. I promise I'll be in touch. Goodbye," Francesca extended her hand again.

"Goodbye. I'm sorry it wasn't better news. Please take care of yourself," Adam's sincerity touched her.

Francesca escorted Adam out the door and watched him drive away. After the door was closed, she sat down on the floor as she stared at the photos of Damien's life. How could her life with the one man she truly loved been such a lie? Was she that naïve or just stupid to overlook the signs? How could she ever be able to face her friends? They were her friends, but she felt a level of respect would be lost between them. Francesca had once again experienced that for a little attention she had to go through abuse in her intimate relationships.

She tried to think of Damien's past actions that she should have suspected. Finally, several events came to her mind. Tina had to be the sick relative, Tina's mandatory appearance at his father's birthday party, and his sudden trips out of town. Francesca was so angry at herself. She cried hysterically realizing she had been a deacon's mistress for nearly a year!

CHAPTER
TWENTY-ONE

Several months had passed since Francesca found out Damien's true identity. Her new career was going well but at times she did miss her former life in Atlanta. The baby was due in a couple of months. She decided it was time to contact Damien. Francesca called Adam instructing him to inform Damien of the situation. For the next few days, she stayed busy with her job and decorated the nursery. The doorbell rang, she was surprised to see Brian. He had finished a case and decided to take some time off. She was glad to see him but was suspicious of the timing of his trip. During their last phone conversation, she had informed him the investigator would be contacting Damien. She had to wonder if that was the true reason for his visit. Did he think she wouldn't be able to handle the reaction or she might turn into Fatal Attraction on Damien's family? Francesca confronted Brian to come clean with his true motives. He stated he thought his pregnant sister could use his help. She gave him a hug then thanked him for his generosity. They enjoyed a pleasant evening in her backyard overlooking the Ashley River during sunset. Francesca had felt lucky in finding such a marvelous place. A former classmate's parents had given her an amazing deal. Her place was a red checkered brick one story which was only a decade old. She was glad it had three bedrooms which would fit her baby, a guest, and herself nicely. Francesca due to her condition had hired a yard person to mow the grass and tend to the shrubs lining the walkway to the front door.

The next day they were putting Winne the Pooh decals on the nursery walls when the phone rang. Adam requested to see Francesca to give her an update. After hanging up the phone she told Brian they needed to clean up before Adam arrived. Brian offered to leave during the meeting, but Francesca felt she might need his support. Soon they heard the doorbell. She opened the door and escorted Adam to the living room. Francesca introduced the two men then Adam took out a file.

"I was able to speak with Damien after he left work in the parking lot. At first, he wouldn't admit being acquainted with you. But when I explained the circumstances and how discreet you were trying to be, he finally admitted his relationship with you partially," Adam's expression was solemn.

"What did he say about the baby?" Francesca was anxious with anticipation.

"I gave him your phone number, but he just put it in his pocket without looking at it. He felt because he wasn't involved with the initial decision, that it isn't his problem. He said you decided to move here and keep the baby on your own," Adam's delivery of this news appeared to Francesca that it truly annoyed him.

"I can't believe he would turn his back on his own child. I wasn't going to let Tina and her kids find out. Charleston is a big city. We probably would never cross paths. What should I do?" She wanted reassurance on her next move.

"I normally don't give advice to clients. But since Brian is Sam Clark's friend, here it is. I would serve Damien with paternity papers. Stop trying to protect everyone in his family. He had this double life, and it came with serious consequences. You need to look out for the future of your child!" Adam's forthrightness surprised her.

"I'm not a vindictive person but maybe you're right, Adam. What do you think, Brian?" Francesca was preparing herself for his blunt honesty.

"Sue the SOB! I'll gladly call Sam to draw up the papers. I would do it myself, but I'm not licensed in South Carolina," Brian stood up and replied sternly.

"Fine. I guess we're all-in agreement. Once Mr. Clark draws up the papers, serve him!" she proclaimed.

"Where do you want him served?" he inquired.

"Wherever he is at when the papers are ready," she responded with vengeance.

"I'll give you a call when it has been completed," Adam concluded.

Adam said goodbye to Francesca and Brian. She sat on the sofa and stared with disbelief. Brian didn't comment. The rest of the day was filled with casual conversation between them. They had a pleasant visit sightseeing during the weekend. On Monday Brian followed Francesca to the Broad Street law office to sign the papers. Brian stayed to visit with Sam while she returned to work. That evening when they returned to her place after meeting for dinner, she noticed there were over ten hang-ups on her machine. She did have one message from Adam that he had served Damien papers at his house. Francesca and Brian looked at each other as they realized the hang-ups were probably from Damien.

The next morning Francesca heard the phone ring as Brian was packing his car. It was Damien demanding to meet with her. At first, she told him to contact her lawyer but after he calmed down, she agreed. They arranged to see each other at her place. She quickly hung up the phone before Brian came back inside. Francesca felt it would be better to tell Brian after he returned to Atlanta. She knew he would insist on protecting her by being part of the meeting. Brian did a final check for his items when he returned inside. They both left her place after giving each other a hug then exited her driveway.

Francesca had to keep herself focused on her job. She was glad when her shift was over. Quickly, she hopped on the Crosstown to I-26 towards North Charleston. The traffic flow was mild until the Montague exit for the Charlestown Mall. Her mind was detouring into various directions as she rehearsed her speech for Damien while in traffic. Maybe it was her impatience, but it seemed as though the cars were in slow motion as she exited onto I-526 towards Savannah. She was glad it was only one exit. In fifteen minutes, the man she had loved so unconditionally but had so deeply betrayed, would be face-to-face with her. She began almost hyperventilating as she made the left turn onto Ryan's Bluff Road towards her cul-de-sac. She prayed he wouldn't be waiting for her in the driveway. Francesca was relieved not to see his car when she arrived home. She briskly walked inside and had just changed her clothes when she heard the doorbell. Francesca looked at her oversized body not feeling attractive while she fluffed her hair before opening the door. Damien was dressed in business attire. He followed her to the living room. He didn't sit next to her on the sofa but instead sat on the armchair. They exchanged polite greetings to each other. Her face began to feel flushed at his touch of her skin during their handshake. She noticed Damien had the papers with him.

"How are you doing Francesca?" Damien used his business tone.

"I feel tired most of the time but I'm doing well physically," Francesca was attempting to keep her mixed sentiments towards him pacified.

"You really screwed up things with Tina and the boys. Why did you have to serve me, especially at my house? You could have told me sooner about your condition," he was portraying the attitude of a victim.

"I tried to tell you in Atlanta, but you refused to see me. Then you crept out of town like a criminal. I'm sorry if Tina got hurt during this situation but you should have just listened to Mr. Sears when you were first contacted." She wasn't going to allow him to put the blame on her.

"Don't worry about Tina. I told her the papers had to do with a car accident in Atlanta and the driver was suing me for damages. She should calm down after a few days." Damien's deceptive actions were once again displayed.

"Why didn't you tell me the truth about your life? All I ever did was give you my love and understanding through all our break-ups. I thought you cared about me especially after our first baby's death and the attack on me," Francesca displayed a questioning look towards him.

"It was something that happened, and it wasn't supposed to get so complicated." Damien kept his business tone demeanor.

"You were married and answered a Personal ad! How can that stay simple?" Francesca stood up suddenly and glared at him. She composed herself by sitting down.

"I'm glad you changed your mind and contacted me." She was aiming to be civil towards him.

"You really didn't give me much of a choice. I've talked to a lawyer and I want to find out how much this costs me to go away?" His offensive option exasperated her.

"In case you haven't noticed I'm due soon and it is too late for an abortion!" Francesca sarcastically responded.

"I realize you're going to have it. But I can't be a part of it," Damien adamantly replied.

"I'm not asking for you to leave Tina. I've been trying to protect her through this whole thing. I thought you had the right to the truth. If you had been nicer to Mr. Sears when you were first informed, I wouldn't have served you papers!" Francesca quickly tried to justify her actions.

"If you really want to protect Tina then just give me an amount to make this nightmare go away. Think of the baby, it is going be tough being a single parent," Damien's repulsive demand was beyond belief for her.

"I'm not selling the secret of my baby's father to the highest bidder!" Francesca's enragement was evident as her voice extended to a high pitch.

"Once I walk out that door that's it. The offer is gone. I can afford to pay lawyers and have legal connections, so I'll never have to submit to any paternity tests. I can make your life extremely difficult or we can close this subject with everyone benefiting from it. It's your decision, Francesca."

His harsh negotiating tactics made her re-examine the pending situation. "Damien, you're absolutely right. I can't afford a long court battle and I'm not going to have our baby's name dragged through the mud. I want to be fair. Why don't you give me an offer?" Francesca's change in her outlook didn't appear to phase Damien.

"Let me write it down for you," Damien handed her a piece of paper.

"That's fine but I'm sure you aren't carrying that kind of money with you. You aren't going to write a check with my name on it." Francesca was trying to not show her emotions of repugnance.

"I'll contact Mr. Sears and give the money to him. Does that plan meet with your approval? I have to leave before rush hour traffic becomes too heavy." He stood up and moved towards the door.

"I agree with your plan. Do you want to be informed after the birth?" She was striving to give him one last chance of a redeeming quality.

"No. I told you once I leave out your door that's it for any direct contact between us. Goodbye Francesca." Damien adjourned his business with her.

"Goodbye Damien," Francesca solemnly stated.

She watched him go out of the door. Francesca couldn't believe that he had sold away his rights as a father. She felt guilty accepting the money, but she had to agree he was right about single parenting being expensive. Her emotions could be released. She cried profusely causing her to hyperventilate. Then Francesca began to feel pains and grasped her stomach. She tried to stand up, but the pain was too intense. Francesca reached for the phone and dialed 911. She awkwardly dragged her body to unlock the front door. Her praying could be heard as the ambulance crew came. Within moments of arriving at the hospital, she was giving birth after intense screams of pain and no drugs for her relief. Francesca was concerned for her baby's health as the doctors whisked her child away. She was congratulated on her new baby girl, but the baby would need to stay in isolation due to her premature delivery. The nurse asked for the name of the emergency contact. Francesca wished she could have said Damien, but that part of her life was over. She gave Brian's pager number thinking he would still be on the road back to Atlanta.

A couple of hours later Francesca heard a knock on her hospital door. She looked up to see Brian with a stuffed bear holding a pink balloon. He immediately gave her a hug and kiss. Brian stated he had a late start since he had stayed to have lunch with Sam. Francesca then announced her baby's name was Jazmine Stefani. She told Brian about her encounter with Damien and that shortly afterwards she went into premature labor. He shook his head, but it was obvious from her expression she had regretted her decision to see Damien.

Brian proceeded to make phone calls for Francesca with the announcement of the baby's arrival. The nurse came by to invite Francesca to see her daughter. Brian pushed Francesca in her wheelchair to the nursery. Her eyes glazed at this frail petite infant. Her throat began choking up as she wondered if she would be worthy of caring for this new human by herself. Francesca placed her hand on the viewing glass as her heart was overwhelmed with a kind of love she had never experienced. Her baby wept softly confirming the miracle of life. Brian put his hand on Francesca's shoulder while she cried tears of joy while staring at Jazmine.

CHAPTER TWENTY-TWO

They waited with anticipation for her to appear around the curve. Then the roar of the crowd became deafening as the children could be seen. Her tall slender six-year-old body's speed was increasing as she came closer to the end of the course. Soon she was the third runner sprinting across the finish line for The Kid's Run 2001 with her wavy brown hair pulled back into a ponytail hitting the back of her neck. Hearing the screams of her name, "Jazmine," she jerked her head to see her trio of supporters. The race volunteer gave her a fresh bottle of water and directed her to the stage. It was a beautiful spring day in I'On Park. The traffic hadn't been heavy crossing the Silas N. Pearman Bridge into Mt. Pleasant.

Francesca was anxious as the race started, observing her little girl run over the small bridge towards the wooded course of the I'On. However, she was full of pride as she watched Jazmine on the stage accept her third place trophy for The Kid's Run. The ceremony had ended as Jazmine ran to the open arms of the well-toned thirty-one-year-old male as she yelled "Uncle Kenny." They embraced then she received congratulatory hugs from her mother and Brian. Francesca and Jazmine hadn't expected Kenny's arrival until the evening. Luckily, he had been able to see the beginning of the race. Kenny still lived in Atlanta and had just completed his fifth and final year of residency. In a week he would be starting his new job as a Pediatric Neurosurgeon at Egleston Children's Hospital, one of two pediatric trauma centers in Georgia. He was excited to be working at the only Pediatric Level I and Level II Trauma Centers in that state. Francesca was proud of Kenny's work in his past residency with TBI (Traumatic Brain Injury), tumors, and seizures in children. She knew with his drive he would have a successful career in this specialized field. He was still single stating his career occupied his time.

They went to Jazmine's favorite rib place in Mt. Pleasant to celebrate for an early dinner. Kenny had come to Charleston to race with Francesca in The Cooper River Bridge Run scheduled for the next day. Brian and Jazmine would be their cheering section. Over the years, Francesca had gone from a size sixteen to a size ten and felt she would do decent in the race. The four had a wonderful time visiting during the meal as time went by quickly. It was decided they needed to get on their way to the North area due to the extra traffic from the race and Azalea Festival visitors. Jazmine begged to ride with Uncle Kenny in his black Audi sedan. He had always been a safe driver, so Francesca agreed. Brian rode back in Francesca's car.

As they sat in traffic, she couldn't believe it had over been six years since the birth of Jazmine. Her life had changed drastically several years ago when her father died in a car accident shortly after her mother had passed away from cancer. Francesca inherited several million dollars from their estate. She owned a luxurious house on the water in The Hamlets in the northern part of Charleston. She had become a successful psychologist in her private practice. Jazmine was a healthy six-year-old attending Divine Redeemer School in Hanahan. She was taller than most girls her age standing at four feet and three inches. Francesca never thought her life would have turned out this way. She had been through emotional turmoil Jazmine's first year with her numerous surgeries from her premature birth. Luckily, Francesca was able to survive with Damien's money. At least Damien had inadvertently provided for his daughter. Francesca would always be grateful to him. The only part of her life that hadn't changed was her marital status. She had offers over the years but after Damien she could never allow herself to fall in love again. Every time she looked at her daughter's mocha complexion and the shape of her brown eyes, she remembered the love she once shared with him. Francesca had vaguely told Jazmine about Damien's existence but spared her the details of his true family life.

Finally, they had arrived at the College Park Road exit for I-26 westbound. She made the right turn then continued to the light at Crowfield Plantation. They were passing Stratford High School then the right into The Hamlets in Goose Creek. Within five minutes she was driving her new silver Mercedes into her driveway parking it next to Brian's black BMW. Kenny pulled in the spacious parking area beside her. Jazmine raced up one side of the stairs while Kenny raced up the other side as they met at the center staircase to the main entrance of the three-story red brick house highlighted by huge white columns resembling Colonial times. The main door had a stained-glass design overhead along with the sides. The outer door was bordered by dark wood. Black shutters emphasized the large oval picture windows. Her house was pure Charleston complete with the palmetto trees in the yard. Francesca's favorite spot was sitting on the second level with the white balcony leading to the white stair railing to the front yard.

The next morning Kenny was knocking on Francesca's bedroom door at 4 am. She unenthusiastically greeted him with one eye opened in her nightshirt and shorts. He stated in thirty minutes they would leave. She dragged herself into the shower and then dressed in her race outfit. Francesca found Kenny in the kitchen had prepared a breakfast shake for her. They took their drinks with them to Kenny's car for their journey to The Peninsula. Traffic wasn't bad until he took the East Bay/Morrison Drive exit and was stuck behind one of the race transport buses. Eventually, they made it to the parking garage on Calhoun Street near The Aquarium. The crowd had begun to line up for the buses to take the runners to the starting line in Mt. Pleasant. Francesca and Kenny were able to sit next to each other on the bus. She still felt sleepy and closed her eyes as she leaned against Kenny's muscular shoulder. He nudged her as the bus stopped at the unloading zone.

The masses were leading them to the starting line on Coleman Boulevard through the lighted street. The two found a good spot to sit behind the Elite runners' area barrier until daylight appeared. As the sunrise was seen Francesca hoped Brian had been able to wake Jazmine without any issues on a Saturday morning. When Francesca first announced she would be doing the race, Brian immediately promised he would be there to cheer with Jazmine providing he wasn't involved in a trial. A few months later Kenny volunteered to run beside her once he had confirmed his start date at the hospital. Francesca was amazed how blessed she was to have these caring men in her life! Brian was still part of the same law firm on Peachtree Street. He had been engaged but broke it off when he discovered his fiancée was being unfaithful. Brian claimed he wasn't in a hurry to commit to another romantic relationship.

There barely was enough space between the runners as The Star-Spangled Banner was heard over the P.A. system. Kenny gave Francesca a wink and a smile as he grabbed her hand briefly to wish her luck. There was a delay in their start as the Elite Group began the race after the loud siren signified the official beginning. Francesca felt motivated as Kenny ran beside her as they crossed the Silas N. Pearman Bridge. She knew he could have gone faster but was touched by his dedication that she completed her first race. The finish line was within their sight as they made the left turn onto Calhoun Street. She got a sudden burst of energy as they crossed the finish line. Volunteers were directing them to go to Marion Square Park. They had prearranged to meet Brian and Jazmine at the base of the statue of John C. Calhoun facing the old Citadel in the park. The two arrived to smiling faces and hugs from their supporters. Brian announced they had completed the race in less than an hour. Francesca was ecstatic about their positive results. She suddenly gave a long joyful hug and kiss to Kenny on the lips.

Her spontaneous actions brought his surprised wide-eyed expression. Francesca jumped back after she realized her excitement might have crossed the line for their current relationship status. Luckily, Brian and Jazmine had been looking the other way towards the vendors in the park at the time. She prayed Kenny would see it as an action done in the heat of the moment. He didn't give any comment. The four visited the vendors then decided that all the Charleston restaurants would be impossible to get a table. They planned to go to eat at the ribs place near Northwoods Mall. Francesca debated if she should ride alone with Kenny or switch with Jazmine to be in Brian's car. Her decision was to do the adult thing. She was nervous as Kenny quietly drove up East Bay to enter I-26 westbound.

"Do you want to discuss the elephant in the car?" Francesca attempted to be humorous.

"Are you referring to the stink in my car from our hot sweaty bodies or the death grip hug or the passionate kiss you gave me?" Kenny sarcastically replied.

"I want to apologize. I was overcome by joy in you assisting me at such good timing for the race!" She hoped he would overlook this one indiscretion from her.

199

"Are you sure that's all it was?" His faint smile made it unclear to her if he was serious or not.

"We have been close friends for a long time. My daughter adores you. I hope this one moment won't ruin our relationship. Can we just forget it?" Francesca patiently waited for his response.

"I would be a lousy friend if I let one incident erase our relationship. But I'm a guy, so no, I probably won't forget that kiss! Don't worry it won't be discussed again." Kenny gave a smile and held her hand as a sign of confirmation.

Francesca was relieved to put the issue to rest as they arrived at the restaurant. During the meal Jazmine pleaded to do the main race next year and invited her uncles to do it. Francesca had seen other kids on the race course. She agreed to let Jazmine be with her crossing the bridge. Brian stated he would be cheering but due to work being unpredictable he couldn't be a runner. Kenny would have to check with his new employer closer to the time. Jazmine's giddiness showed she was happy at the possibility of going across the finish line with her mother and Uncle Kenny. It was apparent, she hoped her Uncle Brian would be cheering for them. Jazmine had another request. She wanted the group to go to The

Azalea Festival after eating. Francesca was tired and desperately in need of a shower. She attempted to curb her daughter's social directing. But Jazmine's excitement wasn't to be waivered. Brian suggested he take her so the runners could refresh themselves back at the house. Francesca gave her approval to his kind solution. Soon Brian's car was heading to Summerville as Kenny's destination was Goose Creek. They arrived at her house; Francesca had always loved her long staircases but at this moment the struggle was real! Kenny noticed her slow-motion stepping and offered his assistance. Inside she took a long warm shower to cleanse herself of the race sweat. Francesca dried off her body then dressed into a t-shirt and shorts. She wanted to be good hostess towards Kenny instead she laid on the bed as her eyes became too heavy to keep open. The before sunrise waking had finally caught up with her.

She awoke to darkness as the phone rang. Francesca sat up to see the time on her cellphone was 8:30 pm. The perky voice on the other end definitely knocked her out of a semi-conscious state. Angie requested an update on the race and her houseguests. Francesca gave just the facts. She contemplated sharing the kissing incident but decided against it. She assumed Angie would probably have told her go with the urge. Francesca had made a promise to herself to never allow anyone to be emotionally intimate with her.

The conversation was short since Francesca needed to check on Jazmine. She felt bad she had slept most of the day away.

Her body bolted down the stairs to the living room she observed Brian and Kenny watching "102 Dalmatians" movie with Jazmine. She chuckled wondering what their fellow "Que" brothers would think if they could see them now? Francesca was sure Jazmine gave her puppy dog look to the duo to sway them for this choice of entertainment. Since the movie was near the end, she let it continue as she joined the group. Once the movie ended Francesca had Jazmine give her goodnights. Quickly, she escorted her to the bedroom and tucked her in. After a few minutes of rubbing her back Jazmine was fast asleep. Francesca rejoined her company. She apologized for sleeping so long and thanked them for taking care of Jazmine. They visited for a couple of hours then retired to their rooms to sleep.

Sunday morning arrived with a group breakfast. Both Brian and Kenny had to return to Atlanta. Jazmine was upset with their departure, but she was reminded they would return in a few weeks for her birthday party. Francesca walked Jazmine and her uncles outside to their cars. Jazmine gave hugs and kisses to both. Francesca hugged Brian but waited for Kenny to approach her with a hug. She still felt a little embarrassed about the race incident. Her thoughts needed to concentrate on the next big event of Jazmine's party.

The weeks zoomed by and it was the day before Jazmine's seventh birthday party. Francesca was double checking her list of supplies and activities. She knew she could have hired a party coordinator but felt for her daughter's events it should be more personalized. Jazmine had wanted a carnival themed party. After dinner, the cavalry had arrived from Atlanta. It had been a while since they had seen Julie and Ron. Bringing up the rear were Brain and Kenny. Jazmine was in her glory as they were wishing her happy birthday. Francesca convinced Jazmine she had a big day tomorrow and would need to rest up. She went to bed without any drama.

The next morning Jazmine was pleasantly surprised by the presence of Angie, who had arrived during the night. Everyone was awake and enjoying breakfast as Francesca confirmed their party duties. The forecast was a clear sunny day in May. They were interrupted by the doorbell when the man with the Bounce Castle arrived. Francesca followed him outside to coordinate the placement. When she returned, she took Jazmine to dress her for the special day. Soon the group had assembled outside at their stations. Within an hour the yard was filled with the laughter of two dozen children from Jazmine's school and the neighborhood. Julie's face painting skills were popular with the girls and Ron's line was filled with boys at the Bounce Castle. Angie was perfecting her precision of a colorful fluff at the cotton candy machine. Francesca was glad she had hired an experienced person to make balloon animals to entertain the children as they waited in the different lines. She found amusement in her grill masters, Brian and Kenny, as certain mothers seemed to be mesmerized with their playful antics and mere existence. The festivities were highlighted when Kenny carried outside a castle shaped cake made by Francesca to the main table. She lit the seven candles as Jazmine promptly blew them out after everyone sang "Happy Birthday" to her. Jazmine was anxious to open her gifts. She waited for her guests to finish eating then ripped off the wrapping paper from each gift.

Before she proceeded to the next one, she thanked the giver. Francesca's gift was a charm bracelet with a heart that Jazmine had admired in the jewelry store. All the gifts had been opened. Jazmine looked around and noticed her Uncle Kenny was no longer a part of the party. Suddenly, Kenny appeared with a new bike complete with a basket. Jazmine's expression beamed with delight as she ran to him almost knocking him down with excitement while he bent down to her. Francesca loved that he had been considerate enough to consult with her before making such a grand purchase. The masses had left during the next hour. The fun part began with the aftermath clean-up. It went fairly smoothly with her houseguests assisting. All were exhausted including the birthday girl. They decided to retire early. Francesca thought it was a good thing she had a six-bedroom house since it was filled to capacity that night.

Francesca awoke the next morning to find Angie and Brian deep in conversation in the kitchen. She sometimes wondered if they still had romantic feelings for each other. Neither had admitted any current intimate involvement. Jazmine and the other guests joined them so that conversation couldn't be addressed. Kenny and Brian made breakfast for everyone. The time had come for the departures to commence. First Angie gave her goodbyes since she had the longest distance to travel. Her children had moved out pursuing various careers. She had never remarried. Francesca was grateful she had been able to clear her schedule to attend the party. Next the Atlanta crew proceeded to pack up and departed as Jazmine thanked them. Francesca was once again hesitant in her actions towards Kenny. He approached her first with a hug as she expressed her appreciation for all he did for Jazmine's birthday, especially the gift. Francesca needed to get over her apprehension of any actions she displayed towards Kenny. It was apparent he wasn't feeling awkward about the kiss anymore. The house was quiet after the hectic activities of the past days. Their routine could be normal again.

Over the proceeding months Francesca and Jazmine trained for The Bridge Run. They enjoyed going to Waterfront Park and running the loop around the Pineapple Fountain on weekends. Afterwards Francesca had prepared picnics for them to enjoy on the lawn with the view of Patriot's Point across the water. Sometimes they would relax while swaying on the swings on the pier. It was a new year, and the race was in a few weeks. Francesca found herself being easily tired. Her level of fatigue was increasing more. She tried to eat more to energize her body, but it seemed to be rejected in the system. Whenever she attempted to eat meals with Jazmine, she had no real appetite. During their recent run, she felt intense back and abdominal pain to the point her body almost doubled over. Maybe she was overdoing it in training. They had to take a break when one day after Jazmine's carpool picked her up to go to school, Francesca almost passed out at home. When Jazmine returned from school, she found her mother laying on the sofa. Jazmine attempted to play nurse by giving her a bottle of water and a cold washcloth for her head. Francesca was eventually able to assist in feeding her then prepared Jazmine for bed. She felt better the next day but after her daughter begged, she made an appointment to go to the doctor.

Dr. Brown's office was located in West Ashley next to St. Francis Hospital. Upon her arrival, she entered the examination room greeted by a middle-aged white male with brown hair highlighted by gray. She was apprehensive as he asked certain questions. During the exam, her new weight was revealed. She knew her clothes were fitting loosely but hadn't realized she had dropped two sizes to becoming a size eight. Dr. Brown ran a series of tests. The results wouldn't be available for several days. Replaying in her mind the symptoms, she thought there was a high probability she was diabetic since her grandfather had it. That was a controllable condition. In this moment, she was going with that solution. Any other outcome more serious would be too unimaginable for her to comprehend.

CHAPTER
TWENTY-THREE

Francesca was on the Mark Clark Expressway, then she took the first exit after the bridge in West Ashley. She was dreading the arrival to see her doctor. Francesca went into Dr. Brown's office. Her patience level was low as different scenarios crossed her mind. Finally, Dr. Brown entered and closed the door.

"Good Morning. How are you feeling today?" Dr. Brown's tone made her feel at ease.

"I guess that depends on the results of my tests!" Francesca tried not to show her anxiety.

"I do have the results but want you to understand all the possible outcomes before you jump to the worst one." His stern voice reminded her of Dr. Stefani whenever she broke curfew as a teenager.

"Please don't sugar coat it. Just give me the facts. I want you to do the band-aid method." She was confidant it was more serious than her original thought of diabetes. Her breathing became more rapid waiting in anticipation for his response.

"Alright, here it is…you have ovarian cancer." Dr. Brown's expression turned to compassion in an attempt to brace her.

"I have ovarian cancer!" Francesca repeated several times while her face turned pale as she thought about Jazmine's future.

"You need surgery to remove the growths and to investigate further how far it has spread." He wanted to reassure her that aggressive measures would be taken.

"How soon? I need to make arrangements for my daughter's care." She needed to plan the sequence of phone calls to be made.

"I want to do the surgery in the next few days. Do you have any questions?" He gave her the hospital paperwork.

"No, not at this time. I just need to absorb this information. Thank you for your time." Francesca tried to compose her thoughts and exited his office to the parking lot in a zombie state.

Perhaps she should have asked more questions, but her instinct was to be alone. She sat in her car trying to decide who to call first, Brian or Kenny. Her index finger inputted the speed dial code on the cell phone for his Decatur number. Several rings happened before a voice message could be heard.

"Hello, you have reached Dr. Kenneth Underwood. I am not available to answer your call. Please leave your name, number, and reason for this call. Thank you." His professional voice stated.

"Hello, Kenny. This is Francesca. I need to talk to you about an important situation. I want your medical advice about this issue. Wish I could discuss it in person with you. I'm also going to make a call to Brian to update him. Hope I'm not rambling too much. Please just call me." After hanging up, Francesca knew she probably sounded like an idiot but felt the news shouldn't be left on a message.

She proceeded to make the next call. The male voice answered immediately.

"Hello, Francesca. How are you doing?" Brian responded cheerfully. She loved the function of caller ID.

211

"Hello. I've been better." She replied.

"What is wrong? Is Jazmine alright?" His voice became concerned.

"I went to the doctor. I have ovarian cancer and they want to do surgery in a few days." Francesca attempted to hold back the tears.

"Oh My God! Is surgery the only option?" Brian inquisitively replied.

"Dr. Brown said it is the best solution to find out how far it has spread." Her voice was shaking.

"I just need to clear my schedule in order to be there in a couple of days to stay with Jazmine." He responded in a brotherly manner.

"Thank you. I need to make a few more calls." She sounded relieved.

"Who have you called so far? Do you need me to contact anyone for you?" Brian tried to decrease her anxiety.

"I tried to speak with Kenny first but had to leave him a message to just call me back. I couldn't give this news to a voice mail. I really wanted his medical advice. Hopefully, he won't be tied up all day with surgeries." Francesca wanted to reassure Brian the reason why Kenny was her first call instead of him since she knew they would eventually talk.

"Are you sure you don't want me to help with the calls?" He offered again.

"I'm worried about Julie's reaction. If you would contact the Peters in person and see if they could come with you to Charleston that would be helpful. I need to discuss updated legal issues about Jazmine with them. Do you think they will be able to come?" She was in her planning mode to be more logical than emotional.

"I'm sure their schedules can be cleared for this situation. Plan on us being there the day after tomorrow. Try to get rest. Love you, Sis!" Brian's support was always unconditional.

213

Don't Judge A Book

"Thank you for everything. I'll see you then. Love you, too. Goodbye." Her response ended as the crying began.

"Goodbye." Brian's solemn voice was heard.

Francesca's tears were rapidly coming down her face as she closed the call on her phone. She needed to gain control of her emotions before calling Angie. Finally, she had the strength to do it.

"Hello, Francesca," Angie replied in a surprised tone.

"Hello, Angie. I need to discuss an issue with you." Francesca wanted to make sure she would be able to talk in private.

"What's wrong? Is Jazmine alright?" She anxiously responded.

"Jazmine is fine. I will get to the point. I have ovarian cancer and having surgery in a few days." Francesca realized she could have eased into it, but Angie always insisted on directness.

"I'm so sorry. What can I do for you? Do you want me to come to Charleston?" Angie proposed.

"That won't be necessary. Brian is coming. Thank you for the offer but I remember how you feel about hospitals. I wouldn't put you through that again." Francesca knew since the death of her parents she hated hospitals.

"I appreciate that you are concerned about me. Just call me if you need anything. Please keep me updated." Angie sympathetically requested.

"I have another call to make. I or Brian can call you later. Goodbye, Angie." She was feeling her throat choking up again.

"Take care. Goodbye." Angie's shaky voice ended the call.

This last call needed to be made for closure. She hoped he would remember her and be helpful. Seven years wasn't really that long ago but at times did seem like an eternity since their last encounter with each other. She had to look for his number and finally found it. The phone was dialing and within moments a male voice answered with a greeting. Then she quickly replied.

"Hello, Adam. This is Francesca Stefani. I'm not sure if you remember me. It has been several years." She hoped his memory was good.

"Oh course, I remember you! How is your child? She should be about seven." Adam Sears confirmed his memory skills.

"Yes, she is seven." Francesca was trying to ease into the request she had for him.

"What can I do for you?" He inquired.

"I have been diagnosed with ovarian cancer. Surgery is scheduled in a few days. I feel Jazmine should have the right to contact her father later in life in case the surgery doesn't go well. Would you please do an update on Damien's current situation? I don't want him contacted." She hoped her wishes didn't sound like a stalker.

"Things have changed over the years in obtaining information. I should be able to do this fairly quickly especially if he is still in the Charleston area." Adam's prompt agreement made her feel better.

"Thank you. Just call me on my cell number I'm calling you on," She gratefully replied.

"I'll call back before you go into the hospital. I'm truly sorry for your condition. Goodbye." His sincere voice was apparent.

"Goodbye, Adam." Francesca put her phone down then put her car into gear.

She arrived at her office. Appointments were rescheduled with her partner. They discussed the practice and how in the beginning years if anything happened to one, the other would inherit the practice. She prayed it wouldn't have that outcome but legally everything needed to be in place. Steve Richards, her partner was a white male with a slight tan and a few years older than her. He was shocked at her news but tried to reassure her during the recovery from surgery he would take care of the practice. She thanked him for his assistance. Before leaving the office, Brian called. Julie and Ron would be able to come with him. Francesca was relieved to have the extra support for when she broke the news to Jazmine.

While waiting for Jazmine at the school, Adam called. He had the information for her. They arranged to meet in her office the next morning. She then gave him the office address in Coosaw Creek in North Charleston.

The next day she took Jazmine to school before going to her office. Adam promptly arrived at 8 am. He hadn't changed in the past several years except his hair had some gray streaks. She closed the door to her private office. Francesca felt she had matured since their last encounter and would be able to handle whatever news was delivered.

"Damien is still living in the Charleston area, but his life has changed. He lost his management job, his white Lexus, and his Deacon position. According to my sources, Damien had a gambling problem which interfered with his job and his car was repossessed. He lost his standing in the church community due to an affair causing his wife to kick him out several months ago. However, my church sources stated, he has been attempting reconciliation with Tina. She has allowed him to return back home with her, but the boys are grown and have moved away. Tina never had children with Damien. On the upside, he does have a new job. Do you still not want to contact him?" Adam waited for Francesca's response.

"No, I just needed to have the information to give to our daughter in case I wasn't around later in life." She firmly replied.

218

"If I can do anything-else please don't hesitate to call me. Take care of yourself." Adam caringly replied.

"Thank you, Adam. Goodbye." She shook his hand.

"Goodbye, Francesca." Adam exited through the door.

Francesca left the office to return home to prepare for her visitors' arrival the next day. On her drive she wondered why she hadn't heard from Kenny. She had to assume his surgeries probably ran late. At home, another phone call would be attempted. As her car completed the curve on her street, a black Audi could be seen in the driveway. She couldn't believe her eyes as Kenny appeared from the staircase. He ran as she exited her car and lifted her up in a passionate embrace.

"What are you doing here, Kenny?" Her surprised tone was prevailed.

"Brian came to see me at the hospital. How could you not think I wouldn't come to be here for you and Jazmine!" His strict voice confused her.

"I can only imagine how busy you are with your job and you have only been there a year. I didn't want you to feel obligated because of my condition." She was attempting to be considerate of his career.

"Are you serious? I will always be there for both of you. Why else would I drive through the night to Charleston? I'm a little offended you haven't realized that yet!" Kenny's annoyance was obvious.

"I'm sorry I offended you. You mean the world to Jazmine and me." Francesca tried to apologize.

"I appreciate your statement. How are you doing?" His expression turned to concern as her weight loss was noticeable.

"I'm always tired. Let's go inside. I have some medical questions for you." She led the way up the long staircase to the main entrance.

Inside they sat on the sofa. Kenny held Francesca's hand as he faced her. She explained her conversation with Dr. Brown. Kenny proceeded to give his opinion and he agreed with her doctor. He gave a disclaimer that it wasn't his specialized area, but he did consult with a former medical school classmate who was a gynecologist after Brian gave him the news. She thanked him for his research and being with her. The concept of a possible negative outcome was overcoming her emotions again. Her body started shaking as she hysterically was crying. Kenny took her into his arms caressing her back in a soothing manner to console Francesca. Soon the shaking and crying was controllable. Her body laid against his chest in his protective arms. The emotional exhaustion was settling in from the past days. She had fallen asleep. Kenny was soon joining her as they slept in their embrace.

The alarm from her phone sounded startling both of them from a deep sleep.

"We need to pick-up Jazmine from school. Her regular carpool driver wasn't available the past couple of days, so I rearranged my appointments. Tomorrow she will be back in the carpool. Jazmine hasn't been told about the surgery yet. I was waiting for the Atlanta group to arrive." Francesca updated Kenny on the plan.

"I will tell her I had some time off and wanted to visit her. Don't worry she won't suspect anything." Kenny confirmed her wishes.

They took Francesca's car to Divine Redeemer School since the staff knew it. Jazmine came outside and was running when she saw Kenny step out of the car.

"Uncle Kenny!" Jazmine screamed.

"Jazmine. How is my favorite girl?" Kenny picked her up in a hug.

"My Mama didn't tell me you were coming." She smiled at him.

"I wanted to surprise both of you. Let's get in the car." He helped her with the bookbag into the back seat then secured her seatbelt.

"Hello, Jazmine. How was school?" Francesca stated in a friendly manner.

"It was fine. Can we have pizza for dinner since Uncle Kenny is visiting?" Her excitement was overwhelming.

"Yes, we can do that. After you do your homework, I will go pick it up." Her mother agreed to her request.

"Thank you, Mama. I only have math homework. Can Uncle Kenny help me with it?" Jazmine pleaded.

"Oh course, I will." He seemed to love her request of his time.

"Jazmine, you must listen to Uncle Kenny's instructions. I will get the pizzas while he helps you." Francesca stated the ground rules.

They arrived at the house. Jazmine went to the dining room table and set-up to do her homework. Kenny brought her a glass of juice. They proceeded to complete the task at hand. Francesca went upstairs to prepare the bedding and towels for Kenny's room. When she returned to the dining room the homework was almost complete. She announced her departure to the pizzeria. Within the hour she delivered hot food and the homework was completed. The threesome enjoyed the meal with conversations about happy memories. Francesca wanted the last night before she broke the news to Jazmine to be joyful. They watched one of Jazmine's movies. At bedtime Francesca gave her a hug and kiss then Jazmine requested Uncle Kenny to tuck her into bed. He rejoined Francesca in the kitchen to assist with the clean-up. Before going to their beds for the night, Kenny gave a hug and kiss on the cheek to her. She reciprocated with a kiss on his cheek. No words were spoken as they gave a final glance to each other.

CHAPTER TWENTY-FOUR

Francesca had a restless night consumed with possible results from her surgery. Her body could no longer stay in bed as she looked at her phone displaying the time as 5 am. She motivated herself to take a shower then dressed in a spring flowered blouse and shorts ensemble. Her wet curly hair was pulled into a pony tail as she quietly walked down the stairs. Jazmine had another half an hour before she had to start her process to prepare for school. Francesca was surprised by Kenny's presence in the kitchen making coffee. They exchanged morning pleasantries and sipped their beverages in silence. Then her favorite radio show was beginning signifying it was time to wake-up Jazmine. When she reached the bedroom, her little girl was already awake and ran downstairs to eat. Jazmine screamed with glee as Kenny gave her a hug and brought a plate of eggs and toast to her. He prepared a strawberry breakfast shake for Francesca. They both thanked Kenny for his efforts. His thoughtfulness always touched Francesca. An outsider observing this mealtime scene scattered with laughter would believe they were a loving family.

More time than usual was spent on breakfast. Jazmine had to rush upstairs to dress and grab her bookbag. It was 7 am when Jazmine's ride arrived, and she was hustled out the door to the car escorted by her mother. Kenny had cleaned-up the kitchen when Francesca returned inside. She attempted to excuse herself in order to prepare the rooms for the incoming visitors, but Kenny insisted on helping. While exiting the last guest room, Francesca felt dizzy. Her body stumbled down the hallway then grasped the banister, she strived to keep upright. Suddenly, Francesca fell towards the floor as she felt Kenny's strong arms brace her before she blacked out. Finally, Francesca's eyes slowly opened to the sight of Kenny sitting beside her bed in an armchair.

"How long was I out?" Her question sounded routine.

"Not that long. I'm going to assume due to your casual tone, this has happened before. How many times?" He inquired.

"Only once a couple of weeks ago. I feel better today." She tried to convince him.

"How much have you eaten in the past twenty-four hours?" His investigation continued.

"One slice of pizza with you last night then the breakfast shake this morning. I probably just need more protein in my diet. Please don't tell the others about this incident. They will be arriving soon, and I should be getting downstairs to greet them." She sat up more.

"You need to stay in bed and get rest!" His request didn't seem to phase her.

"I can compromise with you. Just help me downstairs to lay on the sofa. I don't want our friends to think I'm unable to take care of myself." She attempted to stand-up but was blocked by Kenny.

"Damn it, Francesca! Get back into bed. I know that you feel you have all this extra wisdom because you are older than me. However, in this case since I'm actually a doctor, you don't! And no, I won't keep today's incident from our friends. The last time I kept one of your secrets, you almost died!" Kenny's forceful disposition and glare into her eyes, stunned Francesca.

"I'm sorry that you are upset. But what do you mean about keeping my secrets?" She tried to appease him by laying back in bed.

"If I had told Brian about the threat, he would have used his connections to get protection for you. The attack would have been prevented. Your pain and suffering eliminated. Didn't you ever wonder why I didn't visit you in the hospital? I felt responsible since I didn't protect you from danger. The guilt that consumed me was unbearable at times over the years. I hope it isn't too late to apologize for not being there for you during your recovery." Kenny's confession was an enlightenment to her.

"There is nothing to apologize or to be forgiven. I assumed since you didn't appear to care for Damien, you stayed away. Wasn't that part of it?" She was nervous about this new side of him.

"True. I didn't care for him. Damien constantly hurt you and your life was catered to his needs. I thought you were making a clean break then the attack happened. He crept back by helping your recovery. I tried to respect your space." Kenny sat beside her on the bed holding her hand.

"I suspected part of your opinion towards Damien. I appreciated you not interfering. There was a silver lining to that relationship. I can't imagine my life without Jazmine!" Francesca displayed a smile.

"Your family life would have been different. For someone that is supposed to read people's emotions professionally, you sure have missed the clues in your own life. I should have done this years ago. Last year was a perfect time when you kissed me, but I decided against it since you freaked out! I love you!" He peered into her eyes.

"I love you, too. Are you sure this proclamation isn't because of my condition?" She needed clarification.

"No, it isn't! I have been in-love with you for the past decade. I love Jazmine as if she were my biological daughter. Since Damien you have put up barriers, so you won't be hurt. I would always continue to be there for both of you in the future. I want us to be a family. I can't believe you never knew how I felt!" Kenny's proposal of everlasting love gave her pause.

"You are right. I have been apprehensive of opening my heart to anyone. It is time for me to change my future. Are you asking me to marry you?" Francesca realized she had been hiding her true feelings of love for him.

"Francesca Stefani, will you marry me?" He presented her with a ring and anxiously awaited her response.

"Yes. I'm sorry I didn't allow this to happen earlier." She gave him a hug as he placed the silver antique ring on her finger he had taken from his bag.

"This belonged to my Grandma. I'm so happy. I want to adopt Jazmine so we can legally be a family. I love you so much." Kenny gave her a passionate kiss.

"I'll have to call my lawyer, Sam Clark to find out the legalities for the adoption. I love you, Kenny. We have to work out the logistics between Charleston and Atlanta." She had to make sure details were complete.

"I love Atlanta but there is a wonderful hospital in Charleston. Maybe I can obtain a job with your old employer, M.U.S.C. except at The Children's Hospital. It would be hard for

Jazmine to leave her friends. Plus, you have your private practice here." His selfless actions impressed her.

"I couldn't ask you to give up everything in Atlanta." She wanted to give him the option of reconsidering moving.

"But you didn't ask, which is why I offered." Kenny reassured her.

"How long an engagement do you want?" Francesca needed a timeline in her mind.

"Not long. I have waited for years for this moment. You always like to plan with your lists. After your surgery we can work it out." His compromising nature of moving and dealing with her lists made her realize it was time to change.

"Why wait? Let's do it tomorrow!" She responded with excitement.

"Are you sure? When or where?" Kenny was amazed by her spontaneous request.

"Yes, I'm sure. We can do it in the living room with our friends. Let's check with Sam to see if we can get this expedited before I go into the hospital." Francesca stared deep into his eyes.

"I plan on always being there for our family." Kenny gave an unforgettable kiss which led them to laying down and cuddling.

"I hate for this moment to end but I need to make calls if we are going to do this." She was back in planning mode again.

"Is there anything I can do?" He offered.

"Not until I speak with Sam. I need to call him. My will has to be updated since the plan was for Julie and Ron to get custody of Jazmine. I'm sure they will approve of the change. Please stay in case he has questions for you." Her phone was grabbed from the nightstand. Then she dialed his number while on speaker.

"Hello, this is the office of Sam Clark Attorney at Law." The receptionist answered.

"May I please speak with Mr. Clark. This is Francesca Stefani."

"One moment please." There was a brief pause.

"Hello. How are you, Francesca?" A male voice was heard.

"Hello, Sam. I'm doing alright. Well, actually I have a couple of issues to discuss with you. I'm engaged and my fiancée wants to adopt Jazmine. However, we want to get married tomorrow. Is it possible to put a rush on this?" Francesca was nervous about the pending options.

"Congratulations! What is the hurry?" Sam curiously replied.

"Unfortunately, I have ovarian cancer. I'm being admitted tomorrow night for surgery. The outcome is uncertain. I want to legally make sure my fiancée, Kenny will be able to be with Jazmine. We have been in each other's life for a decade and I don't want to wait anymore. Is it possible?" She prayed it could be done

"I'm sorry for your condition. Yes, but it will be tight. I'm a notary public and wedding officiant along with being a lawyer. I can marry you and submit the paperwork. We can expedite it similar to a "deathbed" wedding. Sorry for the analogy. But if one party is going to have surgery and the outcome is unknown then the state will allow it. As far as the adoption, your new husband will be a stepparent or third party. There needs to be an established relationship between the child and the third party. He must serve the best interests of the child. Since you weren't married to Damien Sommers, in South Carolina the mother is automatically the custodial parent. You will have to sign a document stating permission for Kenny to be able to adopt your child. Usually, after the death of a parent then the other biological parent gets custody. In your case this won't be an issue since when Damien gave you that one lump sum payment and has had no contact, he abandoned his child. Do you have any questions?" Sam's precise instructions impressed her.

"Thank you for your willingness to do this for us. Can you come to my house tomorrow at 1 pm to perform the ceremony?" She replied.

"Yes, I can. I will bring the paperwork for the marriage and adoption. See you then. Goodbye." Sam responded.

"See you at 1 pm. Thank you, again." She was relieved.

"I guess in less than twenty-four hours you will be my wife, Mrs. Underwood!" He smiled with pleasure.

"I love the sound of it. Dr. and Mrs. Kenneth Underwood!" Her life would be complete.

"We need wedding rings." Kenny was attempting to assist with the final arrangements.

"When the others get here, we can go to the jewelry store. I'm feeling better." Her desire to get out of bed was persistent.

"No. You still need your rest today." Kenny's concerned tone made her back down.

"How about a compromise? You take your grandmother's ring and get silver ones that compliments it. Here is my birthstone ring. Take it so you can get the right size. If it isn't exactly right don't worry, I can resize it after surgery." She handed the ring to him.

"Are you sure?" He was anxious she was settling.

"Yes, I trust your taste." Her decision was final.

The phone rang. The Atlanta group was running late. Francesca informed Kenny of the update. He thought this would be the ideal time to go to the jewelry store and for her to rest. They kissed before his departure as he took her house key to re-enter without disturbing her. She heard the front door close and immediately called Angie with the wedding plans. Unfortunately, Angie wasn't going to be able to come. Her oldest daughter was about to give birth. Angie gave her congratulations on her marrying the brain surgeon! She always had a unique style of conveying her thoughts. After a while Francesca heard the front door open. Kenny appeared stating his adventure had been successful, but he would be returning tomorrow morning to retrieve the rings. The tasks were falling into place. They relaxed watching the television in her bed. The sound of a car horn was heard. Kenny went outside to greet Jazmine and assisted her inside to the master bedroom. The energetic girl gave a hug and kiss to her mother.

"We have something to tell you. Uncle Kenny and I are getting married. What do you think?" She knew her daughter loved him, but it would be a change for them to live together.

"Yes! I always wanted him to stay with us forever!" Jazmine hugged Kenny with intensity then sat next to her mother.

"We are so glad you approve!" Her face grinned widely.

"There is a question I have for you, Jazmine. Can I adopt you? I want to be your father legally." Kenny included Jazmine in on the process.

"I kind of thought you already acted like my Daddy. You come to my special activities, buy me things, never missed a birthday, and always talk to me on the phone when I'm sad. You tell me you love me all the time. Isn't that what a Daddy is supposed to do?" Jazmine looked with admiration into Kenny's eyes.

"I love you, Jazmine!" Kenny could barely respond as his throat tightened up.

"You are absolutely right, Jazmine. He is all that towards you." Francesca showed tears of joy from Jazmine's insight.

"Can I call him Daddy?" She suggested.

"I would be honored!" Kenny gave a hug to the little girl.

"We are getting married tomorrow. Uncle Brian, Uncle Ron, and Aunt Julie will be here. There is other news to share with you. Since I have been sick, I am going to the hospital for surgery tomorrow night. I don't want you to worry." She tried to prevail a calm atmosphere.

"I'm not worried. You keep telling me that Uncle Kenny is a great doctor. He can make you better, right?" Jazmine's hopefulness was refreshing.

"He isn't that kind of doctor. His work is helping children not adults. But I have a good doctor to help me." Francesca wanted to take the burden off of Kenny's shoulders.

"Okay. Can I visit you in the hospital?" She replied.

"We will see how long I have to stay. Let's talk about the ceremony. We are doing it in our living room. You can wear a nice dress." As a mother, she wanted to distract her child from unhappy issues such as surgery.

"Can I stand by you at the ceremony?" Jazmine was desiring to be a part of the festivities.

"Of course. We are becoming a family. I want you next to your mother and myself." Kenny smiled with Jazmine's adjustment to their new life. As he held Francesca and she held Jazmine, they fell asleep on the bed.

An hour later the doorbell rang. Kenny gently pulled away from Francesca's sleeping body. He closed her bedroom door and went downstairs. Kenny opened the door to surprised looks from his friends since his car was parked in the garage. They thought they would get there before him. He had changed his plans to arrive earlier. Kenny escorted them to the living room. He updated the group on Francesca's condition and the morning incident. They requested to see her, but he explained she was asleep. Soon Francesca's voice was heard. She requested everyone to come upstairs. They entered her room approaching Francesca with hugs and kisses. Kenny assisted her with fluffing pillows to allow sitting up. He was beside her on the bed.

"Thank you for making the trip. I really appreciate your support." Francesca loved the closeness of her extended family. Before she had the chance to continue, she was interrupted.

"Kenny is my new Daddy when he marries my Mama!" Jazmine blurted out.

"We were going to ease into that, but I have accepted Kenny's proposal of marriage!" Her face glowed with happiness.

"It is about damn time!" Brian responded with approval.

"I'm so happy for both of you!" Julie gave both of them a hug.

"What took you so long?" Ron sarcastically replied.

"Was I the last one to figure out Kenny's feelings towards me?" Francesca jested.

"Yes!" Everyone yelled in unison.

"We have more news. Tomorrow is the ceremony in my living room. We decided not to wait." She saw the astonished looks on their faces.

"Wow! I can't believe you got her to agree to this!" Brian confronted Kenny.

"It wasn't my idea for tomorrow. It was all her!" Kenny attempted to convince him.

"Really. I guess people can change instantly." Brian grinned.

"Is there anything we can do?" Julie's need to assist prevailed.

"Not today. In fact, Kenny is going to adopt Jazmine." Francesca was filled with gratitude her daughter's future was secure.

"Can we celebrate with special food? How about Chinese, Mama?" It was hard to resist Jazmine's request.

"I guess we can do that." She agreed.

"I'm taking orders. Jazmine do you want to help me get the food?" Kenny needed to get her out of the house. He knew Francesca wanted to have a private conversation with the others.

"Yes, can we go soon?" Her energy level was always strong.

"Please go change your clothes and we can leave." Kenny requested.

241

"Thank you." Francesca tried to give him money for the food which he refused. Kenny gave her a departing kiss on the lips.

"I'm glad you are back together. I wish it had come earlier." Brian shared his opinion he had been hiding for years. His best friend and sister could finally be truly happy in a relationship.

"I'm surprised you didn't say something. You have never been shy with your thoughts." She paused. "I want to discuss the plan for tomorrow. After the ceremony, I will be admitted then the next morning will be my surgery." She waited on feedback.

"Ron and I can stay here with Jazmine." Julie volunteered.

"I assume your husband will be there at the hospital. Of course, I want to be there as support system for both of you!" Brian's commitment always reigned.

"I'm so grateful for all of you! My will is being changed with Kenny adopting Jazmine. I hope you will still assist him." Her wishes were outlined.

"We will be here for you and Jazmine." Julie tried to keep positive as Francesca's phone rang.

"Hello. Alright I will send them." Her call ended. "Kenny invited you downstairs to eat." She motioned them to leave.

"I'm going to eat later. I'll stay with you." Brian announced.

"You don't have to do that." She didn't want to stop him from being with the others.

"I want to do this." Brian stayed as Julie and Ron left.

"I need my brother to do me a favor if needed. I'm confident Kenny will be a wonderful dad to Jazmine, but she does have another biological parent. In case this surgery goes south, I want you to contact Damien. I feel a moral obligation to give him a chance to see his daughter." Francesca gave him the number from her nightstand drawer and Brian hesitantly took it.

"You don't owe him anything. I will do this only if you agree to inform Kenny." Brian solemnly responded.

"Of course, I was going to tell Kenny! This is just insurance that all details have been covered." She patted her hand on his. Kenny appeared with a tray of food.

"I believe that is my cue to give you alone time." Brian kissed her on the cheek and left.

"Let's get you to eat something." He prepared the tray on her lap.

"I'm still not that hungry. But I will try." She ate some rice and small pieces of chicken.

"At least you are attempting to eat something. Are you feeling better?" His bedside manner was kicking into gear.

"Yes, much better. Tell the others they can come back upstairs." She felt bad she couldn't be a good hostess.

The group returned to her room. It was getting late and everyone was exhausted. They gave their good nights including Jazmine and retired to their rooms. She remembered the first day they had moved her to Charleston. Francesca aimlessly channel surfed with the remote. There was a knock on the door.

"Come in." She invited her visitor.

"I figured you would still be awake. You always overthink everything." Kenny observed.

"I need to talk to you. I'm not sure how you will feel about it." She was wanting to be considerate of his feelings.

"I hope you haven't changed your mind about the ceremony tomorrow." His pleading manner was apparent.

"No, I definitely want to do it. It is about Jazmine's future. My estate will go to her including the house so there wouldn't be a hardship on anyone. You will be in control of her best interest. I have one request, that she be able to contact Damien. Brian has been given the contact information. I don't want to hurt you." Francesca hoped he wouldn't feel a betrayal from her.

"I will be able to take care of our new family financially. I hope you don't ever think that money ever motivated me to be with you and Jazmine. I understand you feel the need to be fair to

Damien. I had to fall in-love with someone with high morals! I knew this would probably come up. I'm not offended. Jazmine does need to be able to explore her whole genetic background." His words gave a calmness to her.

"I never thought my estate came into play. Please stay with me tonight. I hate to admit it, but I'm scared about this surgery." She motioned for him to lay down next to her.

"I won't leave you." His muscular arms enthralled her body in a nurturing manner as he rocked her to sleep.

CHAPTER
TWENTY-FIVE

The glorious dawn illuminated the bedroom. His shirtless bronzed skin body encased her from behind. The tenderness of his fingers caressing the configurations of her upper torso made Francesca's yearning unbearable. Kenny's sultry rotation of her body wasn't an erratic behavior as past lovers had done. She felt his warm breath pulsating on her neck with each amorous embrace of his lips to her skin. The velvety touch of his surgeon's hands down her vertebrae brought Francesca to a place of euphoria. He paused with a chivalrous movement as if confirming permission to continue. She slowly placed his shoulders on top of hers. Kenny's captivating exploration of her being exhilarated her soul. Her love for him had been rejuvenated in every sense. She realized her love life was all that it could be. His authentic gestures had awakened her emotions. They laid in each other's arms with enchantment towards this new chapter of their lives.

Voices could be heard going down the stairs. There was an absence of Jazmine's presence. Kenny rose from the bed and dressed. He wanted to return to his guest room to prepare for their big day before Jazmine discovered him in her mother's room. Kenny's attempt of preserving Francesca's virtue was endearing. Within the hour, Francesca and Jazmine met Kenny at the staircase. They descended into the kitchen joining the others. After breakfast, the group dispensed for various destinations. Francesca, Julie, and Jazmine shopped for dresses and picked up flowers from the florist. Kenny, Brian, and Ron picked up the rings and bought appropriate attire for an informal wedding.

It was 12:45 pm when Steve Richards, Francesca's partner had arrived. Sam was in the dining room finalizing details with Kenny and Brian. Julie was upstairs with Francesca and Jazmine awaited their musical cues to start the procession on the staircase. Jazmine had begged for them to do a grand entrance into the living room. The sounds of an instrumental version of "We've Only Just Begun" could be heard as Julie appeared in her pastel-colored dress carrying a bouquet of carnations. She smiled when Ron took her picture from his place as photographer at the bottom of the stairs. Jazmine was seen next in her lavender dress carrying a basket of pastel-colored carnations. She stopped beside Julie opposite Kenny at the altar. Francesca glided down in her long lavender dress over laid with white lace. Her hair was swept on one side highlighted with baby's breath. She felt as though she was floating on a cloud when her eyes met with Kenny's gaze. The music faded as she arrived at the altar.

"Welcome everyone. We are gathered here today to finalize the union of Francesca and Kenneth. We will begin with the vows they have written." Sam gestured for Francesca to start.

"Through the years I have been amazed by your perseverance in your career and selfless acts of kindness towards others. I carry these lilies to represent your unconditional friendship and devotion you have shown me. Apparently, you have the patience of Job for waiting on me! I'm sorry it took me so long to realize the family I had desired already existed. I want to spend every day being entertained by your sense of humor, witnessing your fatherly disposition with Jazmine, and your loving protective arms around me. I always will love you with all my heart and soul." Francesca held Kenny's hand as her voice tried not to crack. He took a deep breath then spoke.

"Each morning I want to experience your infectious smile and Jazmine's laughter. I love your nurturing manner and the cute

249

way you fluff your hair when you are nervous. My desire is to share a lifetime of memories with you while getting lost in your beautiful chestnut eyes during our beachfront sunset walks. My love for our family will never die." Kenny's vows brought Francesca to tears.

"Thank you. We will complete the final part of the ceremony. Do you have the rings?" Sam looked for confirmation.

"Yes, I do." Brian handed the rings to Sam.

"Please take this ring and repeat the following. I Kenneth, take you Francesca to have and hold. I will always love, honor, and cherish you as my wife from this day forward." Sam waited for Kenny's reply.

"I Kenneth, take you Francesca to have and hold. I will always love, honor, and cherish you as my wife from this day forward." Kenny put the ring on her finger.

" Francesca, take this ring and repeat after me. I Francesca, take you Kenneth to have and hold. I will always love, honor, and cherish you as my husband from this day forward." Sam motioned for her to begin.

"I Francesca, take you Kenneth to have and hold. I will always love, honor, and cherish you as my husband from this day forward." She put the ring on his finger.

"Do you Francesca Stefani promise to respect the sanction of marriage to Kenneth Underwood?" Sam smiled at her.

"I do!" She clearly stated with elation.

"Do you Kenneth Underwood promise to respect the sanction of marriage to Francesca Stefani?" He didn't have to wait long for a response.

"Absolutely, I do!" Kenny blurted out as everyone chuckled.

"By the power vested in me by the state of South Carolina I now pronounce you husband and wife. I wish to introduce the Dr. and Mrs. Kenneth Underwood Family. You may kiss the bride!" Sam grinned as the newlyweds kissed then Kenny lifted up Jazmine as they hugged her.

The couple was congratulated by everyone in attendance. Sam soon directed them to the dining room to complete the paperwork for the marriage, adoption, and will. Brian and Julie gladly signed off as witnesses. Francesca signed her statement of permission for Kenny to adopt Jazmine. Sam explained there would be a hearing, but he didn't foresee any issues. The couple returned to the living room for their first dance to "Always and Forever." Francesca felt this must be paradise.

Sam stated he would have to return to his office soon. The event was continued with pictures including the cake cutting and a toast with ginger ale. Francesca was grateful Kenny had remembered to have a cake delivered and nobody seemed to mind the non-alcoholic beverage. She hadn't had a drink since her drunk incident at Damien's place a lifetime ago. They enjoyed the celebration especially Jazmine who was in almost every picture. The time came to say goodbye to Sam then Steve, who once again promised to oversee the practice.

Francesca and Kenny went upstairs to change for the hospital. Julie and Ron were going to stay with Jazmine. The newlyweds appeared with an overnight bag. Brain joined them in the dining room.

"Jazmine!" Francesca called out.

"Yes, Mama." She came running from the kitchen.

"I'm going to spend the night at the hospital. I need you to stay with Aunt Julie and Uncle Ron. Please listen to them." Her tone was calm.

"Yes, Mama. Is Daddy going with you?" Her soft voice asked.

"Yes. Uncle Brian and Daddy are driving me there. They will make sure I get checked in." Francesca wanted her daughter to feel safe.

"Mama don't worry I'll be a big girl for you and Daddy. Remember if your doctor needs help making you better then Daddy can help him." Jazmine had a hopeful expression on her face.

"Honey, I told you he helps children. Do you remember our conversation about Papa?" She wanted Jazmine to be prepared for certain options.

"Yes, Mama. I wish I could go with you." She gave her mother a hug and kiss.

"I'm sorry, Jelly Bean, I have to go." Francesca held back her emotions of uncertainty as she kissed her goodbye.

"Jazmine, I love you. I want you to help Aunt Julie and Uncle Ron cleaning up." Kenny hugged and kissed her.

"Goodbye, Mama, Daddy, and Uncle Brian." She waved at them. Brian gave her a hug as the trio went out the door.

Francesca was unusually quiet as Brian's car entered I-26 eastbound towards the hospital. The eerie silence of the group could be compared to a funeral instead of the aftermath of a wedding. Brian attempted to lighten the mood.

"I remember when I introduced you two at the Step Competition at Morehouse. Kenny came rushing from nowhere to be introduced to you, Francesca. Right, Kenny?" Brian grinned trying to start a conversation.

"Yes. I saw her jamming with you as you were attempting to do the steps of the Frat brothers. I knew I had to meet this unique person. That day changed my life!" Kenny put his arm around Francesca as they sat in the back seat.

"I tried to do the dances, but Brian was going too quick for me. Eventually, I got it. I agree it was a memorable day." She smiled and seemed less nervous.

"I'm glad you are back in a good mood. You did just get married!" Brian jokingly replied.

"Yes, we did. This isn't the best way to spend our first day of marriage, but it will be over soon." She had to keep up appearances of happiness.

"We can take a trip after your recovery. I already put in for a leave of absence in Atlanta in case your recovery takes longer than anticipated." His actions always put her needs first.

"I'm sorry you are having to do that. I appreciate everything you do. I love you." Francesca's guilt was overwhelming. She wished he knew everything about her surgery.

"I love you, too. I'm doing what a husband does." Kenny sensed her anxiety.

"Is this the correct exit, Francesca?" Brian had driven over the Ashley River bridge section of the expressway.

"Yes, make the left at the light towards the hospital. We can park over there." She directed him.

"Are you ready to do this?" Brian inquired.

"I guess. Do I really have a choice?" She looked at both men for guidance.

They entered St. Francis Hospital and arrived at the registration desk. Brian offered to sit in the waiting area directly across from the desk. Francesca gave the clerk her paperwork before being escorted to the office. She updated the next of kin to be her husband, Dr. Kenneth Underwood. The clerk instructed Francesca and Kenny they could go out to the waiting area until her name was called. Time seemed to go slowly before an orderly escorted them. Upon arriving at her room on the Women's Services floor, a nurse handed Francesca a gown and her vitals would need to be taken before Dr. Brown spoke with them. Brian left in order for Francesca to have privacy. Kenny put away her overnight bag as she changed to the gown. The nurse returned to complete the primary vitals. Soon there was a knock on the door.

"Come in." Francesca called out.

"How are you doing?" Dr. Brown greeted her.

"Alright. I want to introduce my husband, Dr. Kenneth Underwood." She hadn't informed him of the change.

"Congratulations! When did this happen?" Dr. Brown was surprised at her new marital status.

"Thank you. We got married today." Her face was beaming.

"Where do you practice?" Dr. Brown inquired.

"At Egleston's Children's Hospital in Atlanta. I'm a pediatric neurosurgeon. But I plan on moving to Charleston." Kenny replied.

"That's a fine hospital. I'm sure you will be able to join a practice here soon." He stated in a complimentary manner.

"What is the procedure for tomorrow?" Francesca was anxious to re-confirm the details.

"As I explained during our phone conversation after your office visit, tomorrow at 8 am you will be prepped for the 9 am surgery. Remember, nothing by mouth after 7 pm tonight. We will remove the large mass and see if there are any others. We need to see how far it has spread. I want to be honest. If we had caught this sooner other options could have been used. Hopefully, we can stop any more damage." Dr. Brown observed Kenny's confused expression.

"How long will surgery take?" She needed to have some perimeters clarified.

"It might take several hours. Any questions?" Dr. Brown sensed the tension in the room. When he received no reply, he excused himself.

"Francesca, what the Hell! A large mass?" Kenny's astoundment of her advanced condition was prevailed.

"What?" Francesca defensively replied.

"Why didn't you tell me?" He needed answers.

"I left you a message that I wanted to discuss a medical issue." She attempted justification.

"That was this past week! When did you start feeling bad?" Kenny had to get the facts.

"I guess, last summer." She meekly responded.

"Why didn't you get it checked out sooner?" He was trying to show patience towards her.

"Denial?" She flippantly replied.

"You are an intelligent psychologist. Do you prescribe that method for your patients? How is that denial thing working for you?" Kenny's sarcasm made her realize she had pushed him to his limit.

"It isn't working for me." Francesca calmly stated lowering her head.

"You told Jazmine I was a good doctor, but I wonder if you believe it. Did you think I wouldn't be able to read the difference between a small cyst and large mass if I ever saw your scan?" His eyes peered at her intensely.

"I think you are a wonderful doctor! I didn't want to overreact to every time I felt bad." She was back with her in-charge mode.

"Not sure what-else there is to say. This is a great deal to digest." Kenny turned towards the door.

"You are leaving in the middle of our fighting?" She wanted to resolve their issues.

"I don't want to fight anymore. I'm leaving." He reached for the door.

"God, I hate that! You remind me of..." She stopped abruptly before completing the statement then Kenny turned around shaking his head.

"Who? Never mind, I can guess!" Kenny placed his index finger gently over Francesca's lips. "Let's take a break before you say something we both will regret." He opened the door and exited without looking back at her.

Francesca knew Damien's name was implied in her comparison. She couldn't believe those words came from her. Kenny was loyal and honest nothing like Damien. Her new husband really loved her. She prayed the damage could be repaired.

*****

The waiting area was full when Kenny met Brian. They decided to go to Brian's car for a private conversation. Brian saw the agitated expression on Kenny's face.

"Tell me what happened." Brian inquired.

"I'm so angry at Francesca, myself, and God! She wasn't honest with me!" Kenny hit his fist on the dashboard.

"Break it down for me." He waited for his best friend to be able to vent.

"She has been sick since last summer but didn't go to the doctor since she is always busy taking care of others! I should have proposed last year in the spring. I would have seen her and made her get it checked out. She overcame alcoholism and being a sexually abused victim during her childhood. Francesca started her private practice, reached the goal weight she wanted, and raised a wonderful child in-between. She has accomplished so much. Why would God give her this large mass and horrible disease? I hate it all!" He had reached the top of his frustration level.

"You don't hate Francesca. You have loved her for years. Do you seriously think you would have made her do anything with that Sicilian stubbornness? Your faith is strong in dealing with children in life threatening situations. I'm shocked her condition is this serious, but you have us and your new family. What do you want to do?" Brian overlooked his own emotions to give a new perspective on the issues.

"You can go back to the house and check on Jazmine. Keep her entertained. I'm sure Julie and Ron would like a break. I'm going back to spend my wedding night with my wife. See you in the morning. Thank you for everything." Kenny left the car to return to Francesca's room.

*****

Kenny knocked on her door after speaking with the nurse.

"Come in." Francesca was confused to see him.

262

"I don't want to fight. Let's just talk." He stated as he closed the door.

"Sure. I thought you went back to the house with Brian. I didn't think I would see you until tomorrow." Her voice was solemn.

"I would never leave my wife alone on our wedding night!" He was perplexed by her comments.

"I'm sorry for the almost comparison. You are nothing like that person. I have no excuse for making that statement. I'm so stressed with the possibility of an iffy outcome tomorrow. You don't deserve this backlash of my emotions. I'm sorry!" Francesca hoped her apology would begin to smooth out the situation.

"I get you are upset, and I accept your apology. I already informed the nurse I would be sleeping on the lounge chair tonight." He smiled at her.

"I feel bad for you. I'm glad you are staying. I'm sure this wasn't what you envisioned for your wedding night!" She squeezed his hand.

"I'm where I need to be. Anywhere with you is a perfect night. I will never leave you. I love you!" He gave her a loving kiss.

"I love you, Kenny. I'm so blessed to have you in my life!" Francesca hugged him. She had to hope that everything would turn out positive for their lives.

CHAPTER TWENTY-SIX

Kenny was startled by the knock on the door from his state of light sleep. Francesca had been awake for the past couple of hours. The nurse took updated vitals in anticipation of the doctor's arrival. Dr. Brown entered her room.

"Good morning. I hope you were able to get some sleep on the chair, Dr. Underwood."

"I got some. Thank you for asking." Kenny rose to stand by her bed.

"We are about to take Francesca to be prepped. Would you like to accompany her? I can't allow you to the operating room, but I'll extend a fellow doctor access to the prep area." Dr. Brown graciously offered.

"If it is alright with Francesca that would be great. Thank you." Kenny wanted to guard her as long as possible.

"Yes, I would like that." Francesca acknowledged her permission.

"Alright. It is time to leave. Dr. Underwood, you should take Francesca's bag with you in case her room is changed after surgery." Dr. Brown directed the orderly and nurse to wheel Francesca away as Kenny followed them.

Kenny's stomach was in knots as he observed the staff inserting I.V.s into Francesca's arm while she grimaced. He knew this was common procedure done with his patients before he performed surgeries but his empathy for her discomfort was heightened. Francesca grabbed his hand when they were alone.

"I have something I should probably tell you." Her tone was almost apologetic.

"What?" His curiosity was on alert. He wondered if she had been harboring another secret.

"I have…" Francesca was interrupted by the nurse.

"It is time to go. Dr. Underwood, I'm sorry you will have to go to the waiting room." The nurse instructed him.

"What did you want to tell me?" He tried to give her a chance to complete it.

"I guess, it can wait. I love you." She held his hand one last time.

"I love you, too!" Kenny watched her bed being pushed through the set of doors towards surgery as he held Francesca's bag.

Kenny found Brian and Ron in the surgical waiting room on the second floor. They recalled their past events in Piedmont Park and recent ones in Charleston in an attempt to make the waiting bearable. Hours had gone by when Ron's phone buzzed. It was Julie wanting an update. Kenny looked at the time and realized the surgery was longer than he had anticipated. He didn't want to alarm the others, but he was apprehensive. Finally, the nurse came out and requested Kenny come with her. He followed her to a small consult room across the hallway where the doctor was waiting for him.

"Francesca had complications. Hemorrhaging started occurring as a result from an acute catastrophic event. When we removed the largest tumor, we saw a massive number of smaller ones. The bleeding was uncontrollable at one point. She lost a great deal of volume." Dr. Brown paused. Kenny was speechless at first.

"Please tell me she is still alive!" Kenny pleaded.

"Yes, she is alive. However, we weren't able to remove all the cancer. Unfortunately, we are out of options. She has a Living Will and requested years ago that I sign an "Advance Directive" for the D.N.R. Order. In this case it would be to not do any heroic measures if she went into cardiac or respiratory arrest. As her husband you could petition to change that." He placed his hand on Kenny's shoulder.

"I won't go against it." He wished he wasn't a doctor and didn't understand the real outcome for his wife, but he had to hear it.

"I'm sorry this is happening to your family. We will make her comfortable during her short time left." He wanted to be professional, but his voice strained remembering the years he knew her.

"What do you mean by short?" Kenny wanted time for Jazmine to come.

"It could be hours or tomorrow. She is in recovery then will be moved to a private room on PCU for monitoring. We will contact you when you can see her." Dr. Brown concluded.

"Thank you. I feel you did everything you could do." He shook the doctor's hand before exiting. Kenny went back to the waiting room to break the news of Francesca's pending demise. He motioned for Brian and Ron to follow him to the consult room.

"The cancer spread too far, and they couldn't remove it all. She had massive bleeding which they were able to stop but she lost too much volume. She is being made comfortable, but her time is short." Kenny's eyes were filled with tears. They did a group hug in silence.

"There are options, right?" Brian yelled in frustration.

"No. She did a Living Will and the doctor signed a D.N.R. Order years ago for her." He explained.

"I'm a lawyer. As her husband you can override it!" Brian begged for her to live longer.

"I could but she has a desire for a natural death. I made a vow to honor my wife and her wishes. I couldn't live with myself if I did that knowing she would hate being hooked to tubes and machines. What kind of existence would she endure?" Kenny's heartbreaking statements made both men understand his position.

"What can we do for you?" Ron's sympathetic tone was heard.

"Please get Julie and Jazmine. Francesca will want to break the news to Jazmine." Kenny stated with urgency.

"No problem. I will go." Ron left quickly to pick them up.

"Can I get you anything? Do you want something to drink?" Brian offered.

"No. I'm just going to wait to see her. Why would fate do this to us? We were just starting another chapter of our family life. I'm not sure I'm ready to raise Jazmine on my own. I need to be strong

270

to help her live without Francesca!" He was sitting in the small room with his face buried in his hands crying.

"We will help you." Brian felt helpless. He then patted Kenny's back.

The nurse notified Kenny and Brian they could go to room 203. She was barely conscious when they arrived. Brian left the room as Dr. Brown entered a few moments later. Kenny held Francesca's hand as Dr. Brown gave the detrimental sentence. Kenny immediately held her as she cried hysterically. The doctor gave them their space to console each other. She composed herself to be able to request a private conversation with Brian. Kenny gave her a kiss before leaving the room to retrieve Brian.

"Hi, Sis!" Brian raised a small smile.

"Hi, Brother! Hell of a day. Things couldn't have gone any further south if they tried! I need you to make that call, please." Francesca wanted this to be ended.

"So, you are forgiving Damien?" He wanted her to re-evaluate the effects.

"I'm not sure it is forgiveness. But it is the right thing for Jazmine. Who knows, maybe he has changed." She optimistically voiced.

"I will do it but under protest." He winked at Francesca to reaffirm he wasn't upset with her.

"You are the best brother in the world. Thank you for your support through the years. Help Kenny with Jazmine. I love you. Goodbye." Her sorrowful look pulled on Brian's heart.

"I love you, too. This isn't goodbye. I will be back after I make the call." He wanted to give her some hope.

"Okay, see you later." Her eyes closed briefly as he kissed her on the cheek before leaving. Kenny reappeared in the room.

"The thing I wanted to tell you was that I have an D.N.R. Order but I'm sure you already have heard. I'm sorry I didn't pre-warn you. I had Brian call Damien. I realize you hate him, but I need to give him a chance to meet Jazmine with me there." Francesca gave her reasoning.

272

"I don't hate him. I only met him once. I hate the turmoil he put in your life. I will love, honor, and cherish your wishes. However, I will fight tooth and nail for sole custody of Jazmine!" Kenny adamantly protested.

"I only want Damien to meet her. Possibly visit her at times. You are her true Daddy! I would never take that from you!" She wanted him to realize her support of his parenting skills.

"I'm glad we agree on this issue." He looked calmer on this resolution.

"Jazmine can be precocious and a handful at times. Please promise me you will ask for help if you need it from Julie, Ron, or Brian. Since neither your parents or mine are alive and I'm not in contact with my siblings, they are our only family. My other request is to promise me you will do the race with Jazmine. She has been training for it since last year." She solidified this culmination of her wishes.

"I promise to ask for help and do the race with her." He accepted her last requests.

273

"Kenny, your vows were so pure. I wish we could do one last beachfront sunset walk together. I'm sorry I didn't renew this part of our relationship earlier. I really do love you with all my heart and soul. I'm sorry that you have to deal with all this drama. I never meant to hurt you." She felt his tender kiss on her lips wondering how many more of them she would experience during this life.

"Francesca, you were my first true love and I have never stopped loving you. I can't imagine life without you. Jazmine and you bring a bliss to my life. I enjoy being a doctor helping the children, but the biggest satisfaction is being a family when I'm with both of you. My heart will always belong to you. I love you with all my being!" He waited for her feedback. There was none. Francesca's hand went limp while he was holding it. Her eyes had closed. She was unresponsive.

"Francesca, Francesca!" Kenny screamed in a panicked state as he clutched her body to locate a pulse.

Brian had gone to the first-floor atrium by the chapel to make the call. He dialed the number on his cell phone. As he waited nervously for a response, visions of Francesca's past life in Atlanta went through his mind.

Finally, a male voice answered "Hello"

"Damien, this is Brian Chambers from Atlanta." There was no response.

"I hope you remember me." Brian continued.

"I remember you. What can I do for you?" Damien stated in his business tone.

"I'll get to the point. Francesca has ovarian cancer and needs to discuss Jazmine's future with you." There was a brief moment of silence.

"Is Jazmine Francesca's daughter? It's been over seven years. I never knew the name or sex of the child." Damien's response had changed from non-emotional to a softer and concerned tone.

"Yes. Francesca is in her final hours and is giving you a chance to be a part of Jazmine's life." Damien listened as he was floored with numerous emotions.

"Where is Francesca?"

"She is in West Ashley at St. Francis room 203. Come as soon as possible. She doesn't have much longer to be with us!" Although Brian hadn't wanted to call Damien, he felt relief at having fulfilled his sister's final request. He put his cell phone in his pocket and headed back towards Francesca's room.

After Damien heard clicks on the phone, he waited before hanging up. He wondered if someone-else had been on the extension but dismissed the idea and thought Brian had accidentally dropped his phone. Damien snatched his car keys from the wall hook as he headed out the door. He quickly started his white Honda, and the sound of wheels screeching could be heard as he barely made the curves on Old Postern Road passing the backside of The Woodlands Inn. Damien was quickly making the left turn from Richardson onto Main Street at the Summerville Town Square. In less than ten minutes he was on the main interstate.

As Tina hung up the phone in the bedroom, her face turned pale. After ten years of marriage, she and Damien had been separated for the past three months due to his extramarital affair. They were trying to reconcile. Tina's devastation turned to anger as she realized that Damien's newly found daughter with another woman, who was dying, would ruin her plans. She became distressed as she momentarily lost her breath. She began to think seriously about her current situation. Who was this woman? What kind of hold did she have on him to react this quickly to her dying request? Would she lose Damien? Would he leave their family to raise this child on his own? Since the accident, she was unable to give Damien a child. He had been a good father to her two boys, but they were all grown. She needed to find out what was going on. Tina limped down the stairs as she headed for the door to go to the hospital.

Kenny felt a faint pulse from Francesca's carotid artery as the resident came rushing in when he heard his cries of distress. The resident checked her remaining vitals. Due to her shallow breathing and unconsciousness, the men concurred Francesca was in shock. An I.V. of normal saline and a breathing mask for oxygen was administered. At that moment, Kenny perceived himself as a failure as he was restricted in his wife's care. Logically, he agreed with the rule of never treating a relative, but his heart and soul craved to rescue Francesca's life. Her vitals were stabilized.

"Please God, let Francesca wake up at least one more time. I'm not asking for myself but for our daughter, Jazmine. They have to be able to say goodbye to each other. Jazmine will never recover this loss without it. Please Francesca, I need you to wake up!" Kenny's head was bowed as he prayed for a miracle. He massaged her hand attempting to stimulate a reflex. Suddenly, her fingers moved.

"Kenny, Kenny?" Francesca whispered.

"Thank God, you are with us!" Kenny's prayers had been answered. He hit the call button for the nurse's station for the staff to return. The door opened.

"Mrs. Underwood, I'm going to check your vitals. If your breathing rate is good, I can remove your mask." The nurse completed the survey as Kenny answered his phone.

"Julie and Ron are here with Jazmine. Are you ready to see them?" He wanted her to feel she still had some control.

"Before you go will you please hand me my phone. I need to call Angie." She wondered how to say goodbye to her childhood friend.

"Are you sure you don't want me to stay?" Kenny's warmhearted offer was appreciated.

"No, thank you. I can do this by myself. Please get the others and send Julie and Ron first. Then I'll speak with Jazmine." Francesca's strength was limited as she waved him on.

"I'll be back soon. I love you!" Kenny raced down the corridors through the numerous turns to the main second floor waiting area. He would have to hide his pain from Jazmine. He entered the surgical waiting room giving Jazmine a hug first. Luckily, Brian had returned from his call. Kenny's foreboding thought motivated him to move everyone swiftly especially Jazmine before Francesca was gone forever. He led them to a small waiting area next to the ICU waiting room.

"Why didn't you come back to the room, Brian?" he probed.

"The nurse told me there was an issue with Francesca and I should go back to the main surgical waiting room," Brian explained.

"The issue has been resolved. Would you please stay with Jazmine?" Kenny's mind was racing trying to coordinate Francesca's visitors.

"No problem." Brian sat beside Jazmine while watching the others leave.

Kenny tapped on the door. He slowly opened it. Francesca was still on the phone speaking with Angie. Kenny wanted to stop the pain for her but knew it was impossible.

"Thank you for everything. You always showed me support. I survived my childhood and beyond because of you! Tell your kids I send my love. Enjoy being a grandma, I'm sorry I won't be able to see it." Her voice constricted as she listened to Angie's response.

"I love you, too. Your friendship and sisterhood meant the world to me. Goodbye, Angie!" Tears rolled down her face as she handed the phone to Kenny. Julie gave a hug to comfort her.

"What can I do for you?" Julie knew her gestures in reality were pointless in stopping the outcome.

"Just being here is fine. Please promise me you will help Kenny with Jazmine. Thank you for being there for the good and bad times," Francesca whispered to Julie.

"I promise. Thank you for being there for us." Julie wasn't sure if she should give her final farewell to her yet.

"I'm sorry I will miss Jazmine growing up but I'm sure you will continue to support her. I love you. Goodbye." Francesca's tears continued as Julie broke down crying.

"Goodbye, Francesca!" Julie turned to Kenny who was standing beside her. She embraced him tightly. Kenny led Julie out the door struggling to console her.

"Ron, please take care of Kenny and the others. Thank you for everything. I love you. I need to see my daughter. Goodbye." Francesca smiled as he kissed her on the cheek.

"I love you, too. It has been a privileged being a part of your life. Goodbye." Ron's eyes became misty.

"I, I..." She was gasping for breath. Her hand motioned for the oxygen. Ron gently lifted her head and placed the mask on her face.

"Is that better?" Ron received a nod from her. Brian entered the room with Jazmine as Ron left.

"Francesca, are you able to speak? Kenny told me to bring Jazmine since he wanted to wait for Ron to be with Julie." Brian was concerned Jazmine would be scared of the mask.

"Mama, when are you coming home?" Jazmine asked anxiously.

"Honey, I told you I have a condition that I have to stay close to the doctors."

"Will you ever come home?" Jazmine waited to hear a comforting response and there was a silence as Francesca tried to find a reassuring answer for her daughter.

Damien was racing down I-26 eastbound. He kept glancing down at his watch while calculating if he would be at the hospital in time. Damien was doing 70 mph as he entered West Ashley via the Mark Clark Expressway and slammed on his brakes as he realized he had to take the first exit. It seemed like an eternity waiting for the light as he listened to Francesca's favorite jazz artist on his CD. He had bought it years ago after being inspired by Francesca's love for the song. Memories of his past life with her rushed through his mind. Damien felt Francesca must have forgiven him for his past indiscretions. He yearned to ask her for absolution. Damien thought his future with Tina was uncertain but maybe he was getting a new lease on life with the possibility of raising his daughter. Finally, the light changed. Damien found a parking space and ran into the hospital but was delayed in the elevator.

"Jazmine, the surgery didn't make me stronger. I won't be coming home anymore." Francesca tried to take a deep breath, but it was too painful.

"Mama, will I be staying in the hospital with you?" Jazmine had a puzzled look on her face.

"No baby, you will be taken care of by Daddy. I will be going away, and nobody can come with me." Francesca paused.

"Mama, are you going to live with the angels?" Jazmine's comprehension of the situation was heartbreaking.

"Yes." Francesca reached for Jazmine's hand and she responded by putting her arms around her mother. Tears continued to roll down Francesca's face onto Jazmine's forehead.

"Mama don't be sad. I remember what you told me would happen when the angels come to pick you up."

Francesca was almost too weak to speak as she removed her oxygen mask.

"Jelly Bean, I love you with all my heart and soul. I will always thank God for you." Francesca pressed her pale-dry lips on Jazmine's forehead giving a gentle goodbye kiss. As she looked at the door and saw Damien's face, serenity radiated throughout Francesca's body as she knew Damien wouldn't be cruel to their child. Francesca closed her eyes for the final time then Jazmine kissed her mother goodbye.

Tina arrived at the hospital proceeding to the second floor. She stopped briefly when she saw Damien through the doorway of the corner room. Hesitating, she feared he would see her. Tina slowly edged with her cane to an alcove where Damien would not be able to see her at the opening for the ICU's secured doors.

Brian reached for Jazmine and gently pulled her from Francesca's lifeless body. As Jazmine turned around her eyes stopped at the doorway. She immediately went to Damien's side. Damien looked down at her golden-brown eyes and suddenly felt a paternal instinct as he saw a mirror image of himself in her. He reached for the chair near the door and sat next to Jazmine.

"Jazmine, my name is Damien Sommers. I knew your mother a long time ago."

Jazmine responded to him in a familiar manner. "My Mama told me when she left with the angels, my Papa would come." Jazmine slowly put her arms around Damien's neck.

Tina looked towards the two hugging. She decided enough had been seen. Tina turned quickly trying not to bang her cane passing the small waiting room as she exited before Damien could see her.

Damien continued to be embraced by Jazmine as he thought of the passionate love Francesca and he had once shared. Damien realized he had made an error in judgement by abandoning the one woman who unconditionally loved him and their child. Because of Francesca's death, he would always regret never being able to make-up the lost time with her. As more memories of Francesca flashed through his mind, Damien could no longer hold back the tears. Thinking of Francesca's music, this truly was "The Day the World Stops Turning" for him.

Jazmine eased back from his arms for a brief moment.

"Don't be sad, Papa. My Daddy and I will take care of you just like we took care of Mama!" Jazmine peered into Damien's eyes while she pointed to the somber profile of Kenny's face as he stood in the doorway.

Made in the USA
Columbia, SC
09 March 2021